Prologue

Apryl Kendall

"Shit! You got some bomb ass pussy," Czar complimented when he slid his thick dick out of me. As I bit down on my bottom lip my body quivered against the cool surface of his desk. *What in the hell did I just do?* I thought to myself.

When he backed away from me so that he could get dressed, I lifted off of the desk and began to gather my clothes. Torn g-string there. Bra here. Beads from my belly chain everywhere. What a guilty mess! If someone were to walk in here right now and see this, they'd know exactly what the hell happened. The messy clothes and the steam left on his desk painted a clear enough picture.

"Thanks," I breathlessly chuckled. "But please don't tell anyone about this," I continued while searching for my wig that he had snatched off in the throes of passion. In the next few moments I had to go bartend before I was missed.

"Are you looking for this?" Czar asked, holding up the auburn wig that usually hid my illustrious dread locks.

"Yeah," I replied, reaching my hand out.

Playfully he snatched it away. "I like your hair without it. I love dreads," he replied. Once more I reached for the wig dangling from his fingers. Instead of handing it over, he grabbed my arm and pulled me into his embrace.

"Come on and stop playing. There's a full house out there tonight. I don't wanna get caught," I contested.

"Fine," he teased before kissing me on my cheek and then letting go.

"I think you look better with your dreads," he said as he gave me the wig.

"Thanks." I fixed it back on to my head. I walked away to continue to look for my clothes.

While I was busy looking for my sundress he had already pulled up his boxers and jeans. He swaggered around his office trying to locate his shirt. I couldn't help but watch his back muscles flex as he lifted up items to check for his shirt.

What the hell am I doing? I shook my head and tried to snap back to reality. This was the biggest mistake I had ever made. I had broken all the rules. This shit could cost me everything, even my own my life.

Here I am, a **married** undercover cop fucking the man I'm supposed to be investigating. I knew he was trouble from the very moment I laid eyes on him. If anyone found out about this, not only could I get fired, but possibly get thrown in prison for botching an active criminal investigation. And if we arrest him, he'll certainly tell my bosses we fucked. This could jeopardize the entire case. Why in the hell did I do this?

"You ok?" he asked. The concern in my eyes must have been like graffiti sprayed on my face.

"Yes, just please don't tell anyone. I'd hate for your wife to find out. I know things are rough right now but you two might be able to work it out," I tried to guilt him.

"Listen, I understand why you don't want me to say anything. I own this club and it would make shit difficult for you if they knew we were fucking. It'll be our little secret." Czar walked towards me and pulled me in, planting a kiss on my forehead.

"This is the first and only time this is happening." I snatched my body away. My words came from my mind but my body knew that I was lying. How in the hell could I stay away from a man like this? I was ashamed to admit that making love to him was better than with my husband

"Don't do me like that," he grinned. Damn he was fine. But there is no way I could ever let this happen again. If my husband finds out he will divorce me.

And what kind of wife am I? My husband was laying up in a coma for the last few months and here I was fucking in the back of strip club. It was bad enough I took this assignment without telling him and now this? Even though him being in a coma is his own fault, I don't want to lose him without talking about it.

"I'm serious. I'm only here to bartend and make money. I aint here to be fucking you. Those other strippers will make life hell for me if they knew. You know they all want you."

"Well, you're the only one that I want."

"Uh huh. I told you this was a one-time thing. Besides you are married!" I spat while putting the finishing touches on my look.

His jaw flexed and he shook his head. "Fuck my wife," he replied. Just as he did someone knocked on the door.

"Shit!" He growled.

Who in the fuck was it? This is just the thing I didn't need. I didn't need any witnesses to my transgressions.

Whoever it was knocked again. This time Czar went to answer it. I looked around for a place to hide…

Chapter 1

Mayeka Anderson aka Honey Bunz

From the moment I stepped into "Sweet Suite", one of the hottest upscale strip clubs in the A, I knew was gonna leave fucking wasted like a drunk white bitch on vacation in Cancun.

After being pregnant for nine, actually ten damn months, it was time for me to celebrate by getting fucked up. It's crazy because now that I think about, I've always wondered why movies and television shows even lie about the realities of pregnancy to begin with? Most women will carry babies for forty weeks which equals out to about ten months. I wonder if knocking off a month is supposed to make pregnancy look not as long and strenuous. Hah, only if these naïve women knew.

Whatever the case, after being pregnant for ten months and sitting at home another two months with a nine pound healthy boy that only wanted to hang on my titties, I decided that I needed to get the fuck out of the house. Being cooped up on the couch watching re-runs of *Power* and *Love & Hip Hop* left me severely bored. And I couldn't wait to squeeze my newly thick body in something sexy and be on the scene to let everyone know that I still got it.

Ever since I found out that I would be carrying *his* seed, he forced me to stop dancing at the Sweet Suite and stay home. Shit, in reality it wasn't that bad considering he paid for everything and gave me the same amount of money I would be missing poppin' my ass on the pole.

As soon as my baby daddy told me that his wife was going out of town with their kids and that he could stay with me for a few days, I told him I was going out. I needed one night away from my nipples being tugged on every few hours. I needed a breather from the shitty diapers, my son's loud wailing and not being able to think for a moment without him needing something. I needed to be free ASAP!

So here I was in the Sweet Suite, ATL's premier strip club located in Midtown. No, I didn't plan on twerking on the pole tonight. I just wanted to see my old friends and get back to some familiarity. This place was like a second home for me. Before I had Braxton Jr., I spent most of my days in here, making money or helping my friends get paid.

One night that all changed when I met my baby daddy, Braxton. I was dancing at a private bachelor's party in a hotel suite. After my routine I found him, sitting at the bar, looking uptight in his three piece gray suit, drowning his sorrows in a bottle of Hennessy. When I walked up to him, he perked right up. It took very little convincing to get him to go to the champagne room.

Three trap songs later; he was taking my number and eventually taking me out. He was upfront about his wife, but I didn't care. I could never deal with a full-time boyfriend anyway. I was all about stacking my paper to the high heavens. A man is just a cherry on top. However, when my birth control failed and I got pregnant, I began to see things differently. Now, I want him for myself.

"Yo! We got Honey Bunz in the building! She just had a baby, don't she look bad?!!" DJ Rillo announced when I stepped in the building.

I sashayed through the crowd in my hot pink, sequin bedazzled cat suit with a pair of silver stilettos. Although pregnancy seemed like hell, thanks to baby Braxton, my titties bloomed into a hefty double-d cup, and my hips and ass had spread a few more inches. My stomach was still a little pudgy despite breastfeeding. But I'm gonna work on that though in due time.

Don't believe the lies when they tell you that you can snap back like Teyanna Taylor if you breastfeed. To help give me that perfect hourglass shape I squeezed myself into this rigid waist shaper. This band had my belly snatched for the gods! But if I try to slip any food in my mouth, I will be sure to explode, transforming my carriage back into a pumpkin.

Holding my breath, because breathing normally had become damn near impossible, I winked at DJ Rillo. I passed through the hordes of drunk and high folks, reveling in the moment. Czar, the owner, didn't allow people to smoke in his club so people typically got high before they came in.

While walking towards the VIP section, I noticed my home girl, Caramel Chanel, making her ass clap on the main stage. Before parking my sexy ass in VIP, I threw some dollars at her and she flashed her bright smile at me. I felt like I was back at home and there really is no other place like this.

"Honey Bunz, come here," my girl Justine and Victoria called for me. Their stripper names were Juicy J and Crown Vicky. They took tonight off when I told them Braxton would be watching our son.

"Hey bitch!" I screamed before hugging them closely.

"Hey boo! Damn you look snatched!" Juicy complimented.

"Don't she! Pumpin' that breast milk got those titties looking right," Crown Vicky joined in.

"Girl!" I laughed.

"Excuse me! Excuse me!" I heard a voice yell towards me. When I turned around I could see that it was Eli, one of my former customers. He was an extremely nerdy nigga. I mean Steve Urkle AND Waldo Faraldo would win *Swag of the Year* awards before Eli.

He was about 5'11 but only 160 pounds. Eli's shape up looked like the lines on a heart monitor. His beady, uncombed attempt at a fade let me knew instantaneously he had not had a cut in while. With all the money he made, I wonder why wouldn't he just go to the barbershop? To further add his lame nigga-ness he wore clothes I'm sure my great grandfather wore – pleated khakis, checkered shirts, faded suspenders and dusty penny loafers.

With how extra goofy he looked, you would've thought he was doing this shit on purpose. How could you walk out of your house like this? Did this nigga not possess any mirrors?

"I'm sorry, you can't get into VIP," Rick, the bouncer said while holding up his hand.

I rolled my eyes and turned around. If this were a year ago, I would have turned and acknowledge him since he used to spend loads of stacks on me. He was the greatest tipper out of all these simps in the club. But now that I've nabbed Braxton Nicks, a sugar daddy that gives me whatever I want, I don't have to pay Eli Urkle any of my attention.

"But I've missed you, Honey. Can I please have a dance? Just for one song? I'll pay extra," he whimpered from behind me.

Ignoring him, I started talking to Vicky and Juicy.

"Get away from VIP or I will throw you out of the club," Rick barked.

I'm guessing he followed orders because I no longer heard his nasally voice. Instead, I heard the latest gossip, laughs and the soothing sound of bottles getting popped. My baes were on a mission to help me turn up tonight.

After my fourth shot of Ciroc, I stopped counting whatever else I drank. Instead, I focused on partying my ass off because I was free like a slave for the night. Lord knows when I'm going to have someone to watch my baby again. It's not like my mother will.

"Are you thinking about coming back and getting on the pole? I know Czar is looking for new dancers. So many of us have left because of having babies this last year. It's like the pregnant virus got around," Juicy laughed.

It was true. Quite a few of us that had been here since it first opened a few years ago had left to have babies. It was as if the baddest bitches were having kids which left these raggedy bitches behind. No offense but Juicy and Vicky were a pair of bad-bodied bitches. They were shaped like Sponge Bob. Caramel Chanel was the only sexy in the face and body one left.

Of all the strippers, I must admit I was the baddest. I earned my stripper name, Honey Bunz, due to my silky gold complexion and blonde highlighted hair. I stood at only 5'2, but my body was plush. Tight waist before I had the baby, big titties and an ass with a shelf so prominent you could sit your drink.

A pair of dimples dented my cheeks and since I was in high school I wore green contact lenses that had most people convinced they were my actual eyes, even my baby daddy.

"No, I'm not coming back. I think I'm over this," I hissed while contorting my face in disgust.

This place was like home to me but I wasn't trying to get back on the pole. I had Braxton Nicks paying my bills.

"Oh, you think you're better than us now?" Vicky jumped down my throat.

Bitch fall back. And no I don't *think* I'm better than you. I **KNOW** I'm better than you. While ya'll are making your ass clap for these dirty horny ass niggas, I get to sit at home and collect checks from ONE nigga. Who eats my pussy on command and dicks me down like a porn star.

"No, it's not that," I lied. "I think I need to be at home with Braxton for a few more months. And then I'll see how I feel," I attempted to clean up what I said. Juicy nodded in understanding while Vicky didn't seem to be buying it.

"Let's get another round," Juicy broke the ice.

She poured me another shot of Ciroc and a glass of Ace of Spades to wash it down. Normally I didn't mix alcohol with champagne, but fuck it, I'm turning up.

The night became a blurry haze of dancing, talking and trap music. I tossed dollars to different strippers who hit the stage to show solidarity and I think I even made Vicky feel better about what I had said earlier.

At 2:30am it was time for me to haul my drunk ass home and crawl in bed next to Braxton. It's rare that I get to sleep with him since he goes home every night to his wife, so I needed to take advantage of it.

"I'm heading out," I announced to the girls.

"Ok boo. Get home safely," they replied. Vicky and Juicy each gave me a hug before I headed towards the front of the club. When I walked outside I saw Czar and his right hand man, also my ex, Javier standing in front of the Sweet Suite. We call him Javi for short.

"Sup, Honey," Czar greeted as I walked towards him.

"Good evening. You're going to have to find some new girls. It's getting dry in there and you can't work Caramel Chanel to death," my words slurred as they poured out of mouth like Karo syrup.

"Yea…" he said, shaking his head. It looked as if he could tell I was very drunk.

"Ay are you driving?" Javi asked me.

"Hell yea. I gotta get back home to my **baby**!" As the words seeped out of my mouth, I knew that he was going to make a fuss about it. Why did I have to yell the word baby?

"Shit," I grumbled under my breath.

"Give me your keys. I'm getting you an Uber," Javi commanded.

"You deal with that shit, I gotta go. Count the books and give me a call in the morning," Czar spat, walking away while shaking his head. I watched him as he hopped in his black Lambo and sped off.

"Fuck no! I can drive my damn self. I don't want a damn thing from you!" Admittedly I was belligerent. I knew it. I just couldn't stop myself because of the liquor. Before I could bite my tongue the words would just eject like a scratched disc in an old CD player.

"I'm not playing with you! You can kill somebody. Give me your damn keys." Javi reached for my silver clutch bag but I snatched my arm away.

"NO!"

At that instance J, one of the niggas that worked for Czar rushed out of the club. "Yo Javi, you have to come here. Some bitch OD-ing in the bathroom!"

"Fuck!" Javi gritted out. "Stay right here. Don't you fucking move," he spat before turning around and marching back into the club to handle his business.

I giggled as I watched his fine ass leave me outside alone. If he thought that I was going to wait on him to come back out here, he was out of his mind. I pulled out my keys to the silver 2017 Mercedes S-class that actually belonged to my baby daddy.

Since my piece shit car was on it's last wheel, he let me ride in style tonight. He had been promising me a new car but had yet to give it to me. Hopefully, he did it soon because while I had some money saved, my credit was shit. No one would approve a car for someone who has no actual job income and racks of debt.

Sloshed out of mind, I staggered to the car and plopped into the driver's seat. You would've thought I was blind the way that I struggled to slide the key in the ignition. I've driven home tipsy from the Sweet Suite countless times. In fact, every single night that I would dance I would smoke weed and down a few shots. I've never gotten into an accident before. I just knew tonight would be no different.

All I need to do is turn on some Chris Brown and turn up the air condition to keep me cool and relaxed so that I could get home safely.

I started my engine and tore away from the club, rushing home. It was a cool spring night, where the air was thin and had a nice briskness to it. I knew I had to revel in it now before the hot ass humid ATL weather hit.

As I drove down the street I turned up the music and listened to Chris Brown sing *Party*.

"This is my shit!" I said out loud as if I had an audience. I could feel that I was getting too engulfed in the track because I began to drive outside of the lines. Let me make sure I keep this wheel straight. The last thing I need in my life was a damn DUI.

Privacy came on next. I couldn't help myself. I closed my eyes for a split second as I got into it.

BOOM! I felt me crash into something while I was aloof and singing along to Chris Breezy.

"Shit!" I screamed. I widened my eyes to see that I had hit someone who was walking across the street. He was crossing with a woman who had knelt down to see if he were ok.

Panicking, I couldn't bear to stop and get out. Fear spread through my body and I felt as if I were going to shit on myself. My hands trembled and involuntarily my foot slammed on the gas. Hoping that no one else saw me, I looked around but I couldn't tell for sure. My vision was hazy because I was still drunk.

I prayed that she didn't see my license plate because it would get Braxton and myself in trouble.

"Damn it! Oh my god!" I cried as I raced home. This time, I was fully focused with my eyes steady on the road. I had turned down the music while I rushed in terror. Luckily there were no cops around. Had I killed a man? I hoped not but I cared more about not going to prison. They would eat my cute little ass alive in there.

This is what my ass gets for being stubborn. I should have listened to Javi and took the damn Uber home. Finally I arrived at my condo near Lenox. I parked the car in the garage and raced into my home, trying to forget what just happened.

As soon as I opened the door, I could hear Braxton Jr. wailing to the top of his lungs. *And there goes my fun night on the town.* After possibly killing a man I had to come home to this screamin' demon.

"I can't get him to be quiet," Braxton said when I entered the nursery. He looked exhausted as he rocked back and forth in the chair while holding him.

"I fed him. I changed him. I don't know what else to do," he said, not noticing that I had been crying. I'm sure my make-up was smudged by now.

"You need to give him skin to skin contact. That usually calms him down," I said reaching for my baby. I reached in the refrigerator for a bottle of breast milk and took off my cat suit. I left Braxton in the nursery and laid out on the couch while holding the baby on my chest. He didn't even bother with the bottle. He fell asleep instantly in my arms.

He would be the only one getting sleep tonight because now I had to figure out a way to tell Braxton what happened to his car in the morning. I sighed and hoped that the police wouldn't be knocking on my door. Note to self, stop after two drinks.

Chapter 2

Apryl

"You have 10 days to repay the money in full that you borrowed from me or I will slice up your face."

My heart pounded in my chest so loud that I thought my eardrums would burst as I read that text message.

"Shit!" I grumbled while sliding my handgun into the holster before I went to get some more cash so that I could pay this money back.

When my husband started at Emory law school I borrowed about $120,000 from a loan shark to pay for his tuition. I thought that I would be able to manage the payments, but since I was the only one bringing any money into the home, I had been slow on paying it off. This particular loan shark was ruthless. As a cop, you would think that I knew better than to borrow money under the table but at the time I was desperate. When it comes to my husband, I would do anything to make him happy, even if it meant breaking the law that I was supposed to uphold.

The loan shark was introduced to me by my sister Cipriana. His name is Eli Roberts and he owns an import business. Cipriana's husband is running for mayor and Eli had donated a considerable amount of money to his campaign. I didn't have the heart to tell my sister that he was threatening my life to pay up. Her husband was dependent on his money for the election and I didn't want to mess that up for him.

Recently I had figured a way to get the cash to pay him back; extorting drug dealers. A few weeks ago I was about to bust this corner boy for selling dope but then he offered a bribe. Normally, I would have said hell no and taken him in for procession and bribery. But on that particular day I was at my wits end and decided to step to the dark side.

Now whenever I need money to pay this loan shark, I hit up Nino, the corner boy. If he pays up, he stays out of jail. If I had known that I would devolve into being a dirty cop, I would have skipped the middle man and started extorting drug dealers from jump. Having to give this loan shark the money was too much. Besides, he keeps adding on more interest, making it seem as if I am never going to pay him back.

"Bitch betta have money!" I sung along with the Rihanna song as I whipped my unmarked police car through the hood. The light blue sky was blending into indigo and I had to collect my coins from Nino before it got too dark. I hated that I had become a dirty cop and I needed to change it around. As soon as this loan is paid off, I'm going to stop doing this shit. And then I need to crack a huge case so that I can clear my conscience.

After driving for about twenty minutes, I pulled up where Nino was standing. On this particular day he was alone, wearing a black t-shirt and a black pair of jeans. With his skin being a shade of midnight he blended into the murky evening.

When I pulled up I gave him a head nod, motioning him over. Shaking his head, he walked towards me, moving slowly. I searched around to make sure there were no other people watching this, but it the coast was clear.

Slowly I put the window and greeted him, "Where's my money?"

"Ugh it smells like chitlins in your car, you motherfuckin' pig," he snarled.

"That's cute. Real cute. Well if you don't want to be sitting in the back of this car, handcuffed, smelling chitlins all the way to the precinct hand over my fuckin' cash!"

"Here," he said pushing an envelope through the window before walking away.

"Uh huh don't walk away from me!" I commanded when I saw how light the envelope was. When I flipped through the cash I could see that it wasn't nearly enough.

"Where's the rest?" I asked.

"It's been a slow week. That's all I got for you."

"Nigga do you want to spend the rest of your life in prison? Don't fuck with me. Run me my money!"

"You gotta chill! I swear I got you next time. You do realize this shit comes out of my own pocket. I can't take from the cash that I give my boss."

Pissed, I turned off the car and jumped out. Who did this nigga think he was talking to? I thought to myself.

As soon as I stepped out of my vehicle I whipped out my pistol and stomped towards Nino.

"You must've forgotten who the fuck is in power here. If you don't want the narcotics unit conductin' a raid on your ass tomorrow, you need to pay up!" I barked while wielding the pistol in his face.

"Fuck! Get that shit out my face. I gotchu man. Damn," he muttered while backing away.

"Good," I replied before walking back to the car.

"I don't give a damn where the money comes from. I need it. I'll be back tomorrow," I continued before driving away.

While riding back home, I lit a black and mild to take the edge off. If I weren't a cop I'd be puffin' on a joint, but we get pissed tested way too often so I kept my piss clean. Too bad I didn't keep my actions clean.

Ever since I was a little girl, I wanted to be detective because I liked solving mysteries and problems. More importantly, I liked helping people. Who the hell was I helping by extorting drug dealers? In fact, I was a part of the problem because I was keeping them on the streets. But I needed the cash. As soon as my husband finishes law school I can quit doing this shit and go legit.

When I walked into the house I received a call from my father.

"Hey daddy," I replied.

"Sup baby girl. I just wanted to check on you."

"I'm fine. How are you?"

"I'm good. My friend Mike has some openings at his firm. You can do insurance investigations…"

Here he goes again. My father hated that I was a cop. I remember when I first told him that's what I wanted to do with my life, he flipped out. The man didn't speak to me for almost sixth months. Eventually he came around but he still tries to talk me out of it every once in a while.

"Daddy, I told you I'm not looking for a job."

"You're too pretty to be a cop, Apryl," he said.

That's sexist bullshit but since he's my father, I grin and bear it. There was no such thing as being too pretty to do a job especially the one that I love. I could be beautiful and be a bad-ass detective.

"Ok…"

"You can't say I don't try. Just be careful out there. Ok?"

"Will do," I replied before hanging up.

At 26 years old, I was still coddled by my mother and father because I was the baby. My parents had three children, my older sister Cipriana, my brother DJ and then finally me. I understand them not wanting anything to happen to me but can a bitch live.

I arrived at the condo my husband and I shared, ready to unwind and go to bed. My husband was going to turn up with his friends tonight after studying all week. And I just wanted to rest because I was exhausted.

We had a small home in College Park. Since we were both stubborn we refused to take money from my parents for a down payment for a nicer place. We figured we could work our way up to the type of house we truly wanted.

Before my husband went to get his law degree, he was a cop like me. We worked at the same station. When my husband decided to quit his job to go to law school full time, it put all the pressure on me to take care of us but I knew it was temporary. Kazman is smart and hardworking so I know that when he graduates, he'll be able to take care of us and give me a break.

I walked into our rickety bathroom so that I could wash the make-up off my face. I hated our bathroom because the toilet was coming out of the ground. When you sat on it wobbled a bit. The cabinet doors were falling off of the hinges and there were permanent stains on the porcelain sink. All the bleach, turpentine and Ajax in the world couldn't clean up those stains.

But Kaz promised me a better bathroom. He promised me a nice home after he graduates law school and gets a corporate gig.

I stared in the mirror checking out my face and body. This was the face of a dirty cop and it broke my heart. My skin was the shade of dark cocoa. My complexion was naturally creamy, so I only wore eye make-up, lip stick and blush. I had a pair of full lips and big brown eyes. My hair was dreadlocked, long and flowing down to my lower back. They were pencil thin and had a beautiful sheen to them.

In addition to my pretty face and hair, I had a banging body. Standing at 5'7, I had a hand full of breasts, b-cups, that sat up perkily, a tiny waist and 44-inch ass. None of that phased me though, because I was happily married and had no reason to show it off to impress other niggas.

After cleaning my face, I tossed off my clothes and slipped in a pair of yoga shorts and a t-shirt. I laid down and texted Kaz to let him know that I missed him and loved him.

But three hours later, I was awakened out of my sleep with the worst news I could have heard.

"Hello, Apryl!"

"Yes, Nichelle?" I answered. Nichelle was my lieutenant and also a close friend of mine. She was also Katz's previous lieutenant.

"I have some horrible news, Apryl," she panicked.

"What is it?" I asked. I leapt out of bed to turn on the light. My voice was still groggy but my heart was jumping out of my chest. What in the hell had happened.

"Is it Kazman?" I asked unable to remain patient.

"Yes. Kazman was hit by car tonight. An anonymous woman called the ambulance. You have to come home. He might not make it." I could hear the distress and tears in her voice.

"How come the hospital told you first?" I asked while racing out of bed.

"The officer that was first on the scene recognized that he used to work under me. I told him I would call you."

"Damn it! I'm heading out!"

Hearing that the love of my life had been struck by a car and might not live, made my stomach turn and twist into a bunch of tiny knots. Worry traveled through my veins and my heart pulsed as if it were stuttering. I prayed to Jesus that my husband would be ok. As I raced out of the door, I called my big sister Cipriana to tell her what happened. She was out of town representing our family at a funeral. I hated to bring her even more bad news.

Chapter 3

Cipriana Nicks

Hearing about my sister's husband this morning broke my heart. I knew that she loved Kazman just as much as I loved my husband. I had to pray that god would see him through this.

"Mama, why are you on your knees?" My oldest daughter Braxley asked me when she entered the bedroom.

"I'm praying for your uncle Kazman sweetie. He was in an accident last night," I replied to her before getting up off the ground.

"Oh. Is he going to be ok?" Her eyes grew wide with curiosity.

"I hope so baby. I'm putting my faith in the Lord that he will be ok." I reached for my beautiful daughter and gave her a big hug. She was a direct replica of her father; tall with smooth espresso hued skin and smile that could light up the world. In fact, all of my babies looked him.

Speaking of which, it had been an entire day since I had last heard from him. I knew that he was busy but how could he be so inconsiderate. My aunt's funeral was yesterday and he never reached out to ask me how it went. I had flown to Virginia to be with my mother who had lost her sister suddenly.

Apryl wasn't able to make it because she had to work. I'm currently an out of work writer who doesn't make much money. My husband Braxton pays our bills. Therefore I was able to travel for the funeral. Since my husband is busy with an upcoming election, we both agreed that I should take the girls with me.

As a courtesy to my aunt I ordered an elaborate flower arrangement for the funeral but had to use the credit card my husband and I shared. Too my surprise, I was alerted by the credit card company that I had spent well over the limit. This is odd since we don't use this particular card except for emergencies. And if my husband had an emergency he should have told me. Our Master Card was one of our shared credit cards that had a $10,000 limit. I had only charged $1300, for the flowers. Where did the other $8700 go?

"Cipriana, bring the girls down here, I made breakfast!" My mother shouted from downstairs.

"Come on sweetie. Let's get your sisters," I said, grabbing Braxley's hand and rounding up the rest of my crew.

My family was my world. After giving birth to three little girls, they were all that I could think of. Well them and my husband. He suggested that I stay home with the kids after I had my second daughter, Robyn.

I fought him tooth and nail because I wanted to keep my journalism job at Bossett Magazine. Then I became pregnant with Zoe and I knew it would be impossible to continue working there.

I'm currently a stay at home mother who writes novels on my spare time. Right now I'm working on turning my books into movies and shopping them to production companies. I have my eye on one company in particular. A company owned by Diego "Knowledge" Santiaga.

"Thank you, grandma!" Braxley chimed when we all walked into the dining room. My mother and I made all three girls plates first before making our own.

"So you said someone hit Kazman last night?" my mother asked. She put two pancakes on her plate with two pieces of bacon.

"Yep. Hit and run. It was about 2:00 in the morning."

"What was he doing out so late."

"Probably had a few drinks after studying. You know how law school can be," I replied. I placed the remaining six pancakes on my plate and then five pieces of bacon. My mother made pancakes from scratch and I missed her recipe. I smothered them in warm honey butter and topped it with maple syrup.

When I looked up from drenching my pancakes in syrup, I could see her mouth twisted in revulsion.

"What?" I snapped.

"That's too much food, Cipriana. You keep saying you want to lose weight yet you still eat like a cow."

Here she goes again. I love my mother but why does she feel the need to count my calories as if I commissioned her to be my Jenny Craig.

"Why do you always have to do that?" I fussed.

"Do what? You're the one complaining about your waistline; that you keep blaming your three pregnancies. It's not their fault, it's yours. You're the one eating like you're a pregnant hippo."

"I am a grown woman. I don't need you monitoring what I eat."

"Maybe you do. If you keep spreading like that, you're gonna be watching that fine husband of yours move on to someone else," she replied.

"How could you say something like that to me?" My bottom lip had began to tremble while my eyes watered. It had been a concern in the back of mind. I've been fearing that he would cheat on me because he rarely wants to have sex with me. But how could my mother be so insensitive.

"Don't cry about it. Do something about it. If you want to keep him and that lifestyle he provides for you, you need to keep yourself up."

In that moment, I had lost my appetite. I didn't want any of the food that was on my plate. My feelings were far too hurt from what she had just said to me.

"I need a moment," I whispered before walking upstairs to sulk. My daughters were in their own little world talking and eating. Fortunately, they didn't notice nor did they hear the harsh things my mother said to me.

When I got upstairs, I stopped at a mirror in the hallway. It was brass antique wall mirror that my aunt got from a flea market many years ago; before I was even born. I had gained a lot of weight throughout my three pregnancies but I didn't regret my babies. And I couldn't blame the weight gain solely on my daughters. I had developed a binge eating problem over the years. Whenever I was sad or angry I stuffed my face with sweets. In fact, at home I had a hidden suitcase full of pastries.

No matter what size I was, I knew that I was beautiful. My skin was the color of mahogany, just a few shades lighter than my dark cocoa colored sister. I was shorter than her too. I was 5'4 and thick. I have never been thin, not like my sister. Growing up she was the modelesque daughter. People would run up to her and tell her she looked like Naomi Campbell or Lauryn Hill. I was always thick, reminiscent of Jill Scott. But after three babies I'm about Jill Scott's size when she was in *Why did I Get Married,* before she met officer Troy.

While my husband is too sweet to tell me he isn't attracted to me anymore, I could feel it. He doesn't touch me or kiss me. We never have sex. I damn near have to beg for it. I've tried to lose weight to get back to my old size but it's too hard when I'm chasing after my youngest daughter all day. All of the housework is my responsibility and I am working on my next novel.

I decided to hop in the shower and wash those negative thoughts down the drain. When I got out, I pulled my naturally curly hair into a ponytail, my usual style and put on a nude lipstick. Glancing in the mirror again I shook my head when I realized how plain I looked. If I had more time to myself I would get a makeover.

"Mommy your phone is ringing!" Robyn screamed from the bedroom.

I rushed to see if it were my husband. Lo and behold it was. Braxton was finally FaceTiming me after I had been trying to contact him for an entire day.

"Baby, why haven't you called me back?" I asked when I accepted his call.

"I'm calling you back now," he replied not really looking at me. Despite not giving me direct eye contact I could see that he was tired.

"Braxton, I had to use the Master Card this week. I decided to by my aunt flowers for her funeral. They cost $1300…"

"$1300!!! What in the hell? Did you buy the entire garden? She ain't even alive to see the damn flowers. Why didn't you ask me about this?! And then why didn't

your parents pay for it? They got money!" He yelled finally looking, at me. While it was true that my parents were well off, I wanted to do something nice for my aunt. I was in disbelief at how insensitive he was about it.

"This is my damn aunt. I wanted to honor her the right way! Besides, why do I have to ask you for money? We share that card. And from what I understand you had almost maxed it out without even discussing with me," I replied. My voice retreated softly.

"If you would look at the charges, you would see that it's all from the furniture store and Office Depot. I needed things for my new office," he replied.

"Why didn't you tell me."

"I have to discuss every aspect of my business with you?" He thrashed but I didn't want to argue.

"No." I simply responded.

"I didn't think so. I pay most of the bills right now especially since you're not working. You sit at home and write books. You depend on me so yes, you have to discuss shit with me!"

"Fine. I'll make sure to do that in the future. I just wish you were more compassionate. This is your family too. Our marriage bonds us…"

"Yea yea, I hear you. Just make sure you pay back every red cent of that money within a month."

"Yes, Braxton," I replied. "I wanted to talk to you about your constituents. Eli Roberts has promised another $100,000 to your campaign. As a thank you gift, what would you like to send him?" I continued.

As his wife, I was trying to do my best to help him with the election by being the liaison between him and his donors.

"I don't really want to get into that right now. I actually called so that I could see my girls. Where are they?"

"They are in the other room. I'll bring them the phone," I replied. He was a great father to our daughters but I felt that he could be a better husband to me. He didn't even ask me how the funeral was, or how I felt about having to say goodbye to my favorite aunt.

I walked my iPhone into the room where the girls played. "Daddy wants to speak to you," I announced.

"Yay!" They all cheered and gathered around the phone. Braxley held it first while Zoe and Robyn crowded her.

"How are my princesses?" Braxton asked them. Hearing him call them princesses brought a smile to my face.

"We're good daddy," they answered. They continued to talk to him while I waited for them to get off the phone.

"We miss you daddy!"

"I miss you too. See you when you get home," he said before hanging up.

"Wait!" I called out. He didn't even bother to say goodbye to me, his wife. I hated where our marriage was going but I needed to do something to get us on track. As soon as I get home, I'm joining a gym and going on a diet. Maybe if I were back to my old self, he would be attracted to me again.

"OH MY GOD!" My mother shouted when she ran up the stairs.

"What is it?" I asked.

"Your cousin DeeDee overdosed last night at some strip club! She died" She wept.

"Oh no!" I began to cry.

DeeDee was my younger cousin, my mother's brother's daughter. She was a wayward wild child who only dated drug dealers. I had heard through the grapevine that she was stripping but this confirms it. We tried to convince her to come to the funeral this weekend but she refused to come.

Tears flooded my face. How could I lose two family members in the same month? I pray that my brother in law wouldn't be the third.

Chapter 4

Aria Brass

"Yes daddy!" I hollered in his ear while he pinned me to the wall, pumping in and out of me like he was trying to put a baby up in there.

His strength always turned me on. I loved the way he was able to lift me up and hold my legs on his shoulders while thrusting in me. He had stamina for days too. This man didn't get tired nor let up until I came all over his 10-inch pulsing dick, at least two times.

"Who pussy is it?" he growled while banging inside of me. I swear I could feel the tip of his dick in my belly button.

"It's all yours," I groaned.

"Damn right," he replied.

My heart began to pick up it's pace as I felt my walls tighten around his girth. My g-spot pulsed like a drum. The cool wall against my back helped to keep me from overheating because the way he was going, I just knew that I was going to explode.

"I feel that pussy coming," he whispered in my ear, slowing down his strokes. He swiveled his hips and made circular motions inside of my hot cave. Immediately I flooded him as if a dam had broken. My stiletto nails dug into his back while I busted all over him. My heart banged at my sternum as if it were trying to jump out of me and onto his chest.

"Fuck I'm coming too!" he announced. Pushing me into the wall he released his nectar in side of me. Thank god, for my IUD. There will be no babies popping up nine months from now.

"Oooh," I moaned when I felt him leak into me.

"Yeah…" he whimpered. Utilizing his last bit of strength, he carried me over to the bed and placed me down before laying next to me. I rested my head on his beating chest while he stroked my luxurious hair.

Just because a bitch's legs don't work, don't mean her juice box can't drown a nigga and have him ready to pass out.

Yep that's right, I'm a disabled paraplegic. eleven months, four days, ten hours and six minutes have passed since I've been confined to this damn wheelchair. It had become my ball and chain but also my bargaining chip. Life had dealt me a tough hand but I was playing my cards well. It was my husband's fault that I was in this damn thing in the first place. I was shot in the back during a robbery. As a result, I never let him live it down.

For example, I pressured him into buying a new mansion in Sandy Springs. This house looked like a castle fit for the queen that I am! Complete with eight bedrooms, twelve bathrooms, a French styled kitchen and a movie theater; it was the perfect house to say, "I'm sorry, I crippled you."

"Baby you gotta help me into the shower. The contractors and my husband will be coming soon," I said to my secret side nigga

Nokio, who was also one of my husband's goons. Oh you probably thought I was fucking husband. Nope!

"Yeah, let's both get ready."

Twenty minutes later we were both showered and dressed.

"I gotta run to the club and handle something. Talk to you later, shawty," he said while kissing me on the cheek.

"Aight, see you later," I replied.

* * *

Today I was working with the contractors to build my perfect bathroom. I wanted a claw foot tub that sat in the center of the floor like one of those old Hollywood movies.

"We can make your bathroom handicap accessible…" the contractor informed me as he viewed the bathroom. I hated the word handicapped especially since a bitch was still fly.

If you looked at me from the shoulders up, you wouldn't think this woman couldn't walk. And I guess if you looked at my legs now you wouldn't believe that I used to rip the runway.

Despite being confined to this custom leather and chrome wheelchair, I still dressed like a supermodel. My immobile feet stayed in a pair of Red Bottoms. Not being able to walk just ensured that they didn't get scuffed up.

When I first met my husband Czar Brass, I was a 15-year-old beauty queen. I wouldn't give Czar the time of day. Besides my daddy would have killed me since Czar was one of his corner boys. My father was the Cubano kingpin Dante Matias whom married my Jamaican beauty queen mother, Ciara Tony.

Together they made my sexy ass; a tall, curvaceous caramel woman with a pair of hazel eyes. My hair was long and wavy but I usually kept it straight. I also added tracks to make it look fuller. My hair is what caught Czar's eyes the first time we met. What caught my eye was his hunger. I knew that he was ambitious. He was the type of nigga that had fire blazing behind their eyes. However, I stayed away from him when we first met because he couldn't afford me yet. Over the years Czar climbed the ranks and eventually became a boss like my father.

When my daddy was sent upstate for murder, he trusted him so much that he handed his business and his princess over. Czar protected me and looked out for me, until one day…. Maybe I can't fully blame him for the robbery.

I was out in Vegas on a little vacay that I begged him to come with me on. He refused saying that he had to work. At the time, he was opening several more strip clubs in the south, modeled after his first one, The Sweet Suite. When he decided not to go I was disappointed but I was determined to shop, gamble in those casinos and get pampered at those five star spas.

Because he takes care of me, he booked the hotel room and everything for me. Some niggas that worked for him, decided to betray him and rob me. In the process they shot me. Two bullets to my spine ruined my fucking life.

Czar felt incredibly bad. Not to mention my father was sending angry ass threats from his cell. My father gave Czar 24 hours to find the niggas that shot me. Well Czar is so efficient it took him half of the time. Before I had awaken out of my coma he toe-tagged them niggas, leaving them somewhere in the hot as hell Nevada desert.

Now, he gives me absolutely everything my heart could ask for in an attempt to make up for the shooting. And I can't lie, I revel in the attention. Every bit of it brings me joy.

"Do whatever you need to do," I replied to the contractor before wheeling out of the bathroom. I wheeled myself into the custom closet that was being built for me. Czar declared the second to largest bedroom as my wardrobe room. I couldn't wait until it was complete.

Despite making him pay in dollars for what happened to me, I also had to make him pay for the cheating he did in the past. The first few years of our marriage was rocky but eventually he became faithful. Unfortunately, I never forgave him. After I was shot last year, Nokio became my comfort and the rest is history.

"Bae!" Czar called out to me when he walked into the house.

"Yeah, I'm upstairs in my closet."

In a flash I heard his steps race up the stairs to meet me. His sensual scent of Dolce & Gabbana greeted my nostrils before I could even see him.

"Hi baby," I replied when I heard his steps pace into the room.

"Something went down at Sweet Suite last night," he spat. I could see the distress written in his gorgeous face.

My husband was one of the sexiest men I had ever laid eyes on. He was light skinned, about Drake's complexion. His eyes were blue like Michael Ealy, and his wavy raven hair was cut low. Those baby blues complimented his strong jaw-line. Shit, it was him that should've been a model.

"What happened?" I asked.

"One of the dancers, DeeDee, overdosed and died. Now the cops are going to be all in my shit!" he barked.

"I thought we agreed that you weren't going to move weight inside the club," I replied.

"I'm not! I don't know where she got that shit from. It wasn't from us. I don't need no cops sniffing around my damn club," he gritted. He kicked one of the many boxes in our home before he sunk into the taupe chaise lounge chair that sat in the center of my closet.

"Have the cops come by yet?"

"Of course they did. Detectives and drug sniffing dogs are all over the club already."

"Well no need to worry. They aren't gonna find anything," I attempted to comfort him.

"They didn't find anything this time. That doesn't mean that they won't go snooping around. They might start following me and the boys. Shit, if this shit drags on, the FBI and IRS might start their own god damn investigation."

"Don't worry boo ! You know I do a good job of cleaning up the books baby," I replied. I had become the person he trusted to launder his money to make sure that it looked like it all came from legit sources.

"Yes you do, bae. I just think this is a wakeup call. I got paper stacked. I just bought you this beautiful home without a hassle. We have cars, clothes and rental property. I think I want out of the game. We can survive, hell thrive, on the money from the clubs. And we can start investing in other businesses. It's too hot to keep doing this."

Had my beautiful blue-eyed husband lost his mind? Did he really think he could just get out of the dope game? A game my father played and trusted him to continue to win? Hell no. Not on my damn watch.

"You're just little shook. I think you need to relax and not think about this right now. You don't wanna throw away everything that we've built." I replied, looking up to him.

"Baby, we've built so much more than this drug empire. And I can build even more. I've been feeling like this since you were shot last year. This shit isn't worth your life. I can't do this anymore. I want out," he said before leaning down and giving me kiss on the forehead.

I shook my head. There was no way in hell I was letting him give up all of this.

"I only came home so that I could grab some documents. I gotta go back to the club. We'll talk more about this later," he continued. I watched him as he walked out of my closet.

The only way out of this empire is through death. I'd hate to have to kill my beloved husband but if he doesn't come to his senses, I just might have too. I love him but I love money more. Those clubs will never make the same amount of money that trafficking does.

This nigga is running Atlanta and he wants to give it up because one little bitch died of an overdose. I'm not a quitter and I'm certainly not going to stay with one.

Chapter 5

Apryl

Still in a panic I raced to his hospital room as soon as I could.

"Please let him live," had become a mantra ever since I found out about his terrible accident. The fluorescent lights assaulted my eyes as I pushed towards the ICU. The smell of sickness twisted my stomach, forcing sour bile to rise. Hospitals made my skin crawl.

"Hi I'm Apryl Kendall. I'm here to see Kazman Kendall," I announced to the front desk.

"Sure ma'am, please sign in here."

I signed my name and received a visitor's badge before dashing off to the back. When I got there, I saw that Nichelle, my lieutenant was standing in the room. Also in the room was my mother-in-law, Sheila.

"Oh my god," I began to cry once my eyes laid upon my husband's banged up body. Nichelle pulled me in and gave me a warm hug. "How did this happen?" I furiously asked as tears ran down my face.

"Oh Apryl, I'm so sorry!" Nichelle replied as she held me. His mother barely moved. No surprise there. She didn't like me very much.

Turning my attention towards Sheila, I at least wanted to acknowledge her, "Hi Mrs. Kendall."

"Hi Apryl," she replied flatly.

"I mean, what happened ?!? Is he going to be ok?" I asked.

"He was hit by a car. The person kept driving like she didn't see him. Apparently there was a witness. The witness called it in but didn't stay with him. When EMS arrived on the scene he was alone," Nichelle explained.

« Oh my god ! I just wanna know if he's going to be alright ! That's all ! »

"Well, the doctors put him into a medically-induced coma so that the swelling around his brain go down. A few of his ribs were broken. It was a pretty nasty hit. We're not sure when he'll wake up."

« Who in the fuck did this though !? »

"We are trying to do everything to find the person who did this. I even have folks in our department working on it. We're not having any luck. We can't identify the voice and there are no cameras in the area."

I felt as if my world was getting even darker and smaller.

"Listen Apryl, you know I'm gonna do everything in my power to find out who did this. You're more than just my employee. We are good friends and I want to see whoever did this rot in prison," Nichelle's arms draped around me.

My legs shook in anger as tears poured from my eyes. There were so many thoughts running through my head. My husband could die! And he didn't have health insurance to cover these fees. How was I going to be able to afford this? I wanted to him to have the best care that he could possibly get. On top of the money I owed the loan shark and our other expenses, I wasn't sure how I was going to afford his hospital bills.

The heart monitor in the background beeped, matching the pulsing of my temples. I broke away from Nichelle's embrace and walked over to him and caressed his cheek. I knelt down and whispered in his ear, "You're going to survive this. You're going to make it because I need you." I then kissed his cheek.

Just as I walked away, I received a call from Cipriana.

"Hey sis," I answered.

"What's the news?"

"He's in a coma right now. They are waiting for the swelling in his brain to go down. Some of his ribs were broken."

"Oh my god! I'll be praying for him."

"Thank you," I replied as a few more tears escaped down my cheeks.

"I have more bad news though…"She continued.

"What is it?"

"DeeDee overdosed at a strip club last night. She's dead," Cipriana whimpered while she began to cry. I couldn't shed any more tears. My soul was already numb from the piercing news about my husband. I swear when it rains, it pours. And right now it felt like I was caught in a hurricane Katrina.

DeeDee was a young troubled woman but I always thought she could get better. It hurt me to know that she would never get a chance. Could this day get any worse?

Chapter 6

Mayeka

The sun rose without me ever shutting my eyes. After I finally put the baby down in his crib while Braxton slept in my bed, I went back outside to the garage to assess the damage of his Mercedes. Luckily there was only a little dent that I could easily explain away.

"Oh someone must have dinged it when they were leaving the parking lot." That would be an easy and believable lie to tell.

However, there was blood on the car, which I thoroughly cleaned up before sneaking back in the house. No police had shown up to my door so I figured I was in the clear. I sure hope that nigga made it, whoever he was.

After cleaning up the blood, I washed my hands and then crept back into bed.

"Where did you go?" Braxton asked me when I settled next to him.

"I left my phone in the car last night. I had to get it," I lied.

"Oh, come here," he said, pulling me into his arms.

I loved waking up to him. There was something soothing about having a warm body in bed next to me, even if it was temporary. Before I met him I said that I didn't want a full time relationship but now that we have this baby together, I wanted him to be with me full time.

"When is your wife coming back?" I asked.

"Tomorrow. I'm not looking forward to it. I do miss my girls though," he replied.

"Why don't you just leave her and be with me," I suggested.

"I thought you said you liked our arrangement. Besides, it's election year, it would hurt me if I left her."

"Well do it after you win."

"We can talk about it after that. For now, let me enjoy the time I have with you," he said kissing the back of my neck. I sighed but gave in. We lay together in the bed with him spooning me, my ass pressed against his dick that poked through his boxers.

Feeling his hardness made me horny. My pussy began to moisten while he kissed the back of my neck. Braxton's hands reached for my breasts and squeezed them gently.

"Mhhhm. You want this pussy?" I asked.

"Hell yea," he groaned. He tugged at my yoga pants and pulled them off of me. While he did that I tore my shirt from over my head exposing my full breasts. His hands crept around to my titties again, cupping them while his thumbs trailed over my nipples. My nipples jumped to attention while blood pulsed through my veins.

My hand wandered to his shaft as I pulled it out of his boxers.

"You know what to do with that?" he chuckled before biting my earlobe.

"Oh you know I know what to do," I flirted back.

Grabbing his throbbing dick, I began to stroke it. I didn't feel like giving him head, so I rubbed my clit with my other hand to get me wet. I needed to feel his dick stretch my pussy out. Despite having a baby two months ago, my pussy snapped right back into place.

When he realized that I was rubbing my clit, he removed my hand and did it for me. His sucked on his fingers before pressing them to my love button.

"Damn, baby," I moaned. My pussy became drench and ready to take him in.

"I need to feel you inside of me," I cried.

His dick didn't delay. My wish was his command. He lifted my thick thigh and slid his dick in me from the side. I sank my teeth into my bottom lip as I felt his 11-inch dick reach inside my soul.

The sun beamed through the blinds, sizzling our already burning bodies. Every time we fucked it was like the first time. With my leg lifted to the heavens he began to thrash in and out of me, forcing my wetness to spill out all over the bed.

"This pussy is so creamy," he gasped.

"Uh huh," was all that I could muster up. His dick had me tongue tied and in a whirlwind.

"Take this dick…" he growled ramming it into me deeper. I swear I could feel the tip of his dick in my navel. My hands reached up and grabbed hold up my tufted headboard while a few of his fingers pressed against my clit. What was he trying to do? The sensation of him pressing on my clit while his dick pressed on my g-spot brought me to tears.

"Yes daddy!" I hollered as he dug into me as if he were excavating for gold.

"Come for me. Come all over this dick!" He commanded. Our bodies, steamed with sweat beading on our skin.

"Hmmmm," I moaned. I could feel my walls collapsing and swallowing his dick with no mercy. My core vibrated while my lifted leg rattled in his hand. I was about to burst all over him.

As he began to bang into me more, I came, juices shot out of me like a water sprinkler system.

"Yea, that's right," he said as I screamed to the top of my lungs.

But damn, my loudness woke our son because suddenly I could hear him cry in his nursery.

"Hold up, I'm about to bust," he said pulling out his dick and coming on my back.

"Ooohh shit," he said as he emptied his nut onto me. It was better on me than in me, Lord knows I didn't want another baby.

After he came he collapsed on his back while I laid there breathless.

"I know you hear that…" he said breathlessly.

"What?"

"BJ! Go see what he needs!" he commanded. He was still winded from busting his nut. I sucked my teeth and got up out of the bed to check on my son. I made sure I wiped Braxton's nut off of me and then put on a robe. That would be gross if I walked in there with that shit sticking to my back.

"What are you yelling about little boy?" I playfully asked when I walked into the room. As soon as he saw my face his shrieking ceased. My baby is such a mama's boy.

I rocked him back and forth while leaving his nursery. I headed to the kitchen to prepare him a bottle. While working on feeding BJ, I heard Braxton in the room on the phone. He was talking to *her*.

"Your cousin DeeDee died?" I overheard him say.

I slid BJ's bottle full of breast milk in a water-filled pot on the stove. After turning on the burner, I went to go eavesdrop on Braxton's conversation. I don't know why I was being so nosey but lately it was killing me whenever he talked to her. Perhaps it was having his baby that changed me. But lately, I wanted him all to myself.

"Damn, I'm sorry to hear that. That's what happens when you become a stripper," he callously said.

He must've been talking about DeeDee one of the new girls at the Sweet Suite. And then it started coming back to me. Before I left the club Javi got called back in because some bitch had OD'd. It was probably a young girl. They are always doing the most.

"Aight. Well, let me know when you're back home," he said trying to rush her off of the phone. I could hear him suck his teeth and sigh. She must've have started talking again.

"Whaaaaaa Whaaaa!" BJ began crying again. Shit. I was taking too long to feed him.

I rushed back into the kitchen but I heard Braxton's footsteps follow. He appeared to have put his phone on mute.

"Keep him quiet. I'm on the phone with my wife," he barked.

I nodded before he escaped back into the room.

"No, Cipriana that was just the TV…" he lied.

He doesn't even love that bitch. Why is he lying to her? I tried to sooth BJ while the bottle warmed but he was cranky. He continued to cry and squirm in my arms. It was damn near impossible to pick the bottle out of the pot, test it and console him at the same time.

"Why were you listening to my conversation?" Braxton asked when he appeared in the kitchen.

"Why are you even talking to her while you're here with me? I thought you already had your check-in yesterday!" I hissed.

"Even though it's none of your business, she called to tell me that her cousin died last night. She died at Sweet Suite, where your ass was," he fussed.

"Oh damn."

"That's why I made you quit. You're not going back to that club, putting yourself at risk. I don't even want you visiting your little hoe friends. If you wanna hang out with those thots, meet them at the mall."

I snickered while rolling my eyes to the high heavens. I repositioned BJ in my arms so that I could finally pick up his bottle.

"You are not my daddy. You can't tell me what to do," I snarled.

"You weren't saying that this morning." He grinned.

True.

"And yes I can tell you what to do. I'm paying your rent, for your clothes, food and everything that BJ needs. What I say goes. Got it?"

"Yea…" I replied while testing the milk before I gave it to BJ. He was right. As long as he was supporting me, I needed to follow what he said. But I needed him to meet me halfway. If he wanted me to keep BJ a secret during his election, he needed to leave that fat ass wife of his.

Chapter 7

Cipriana

A couple of days had passed since the funeral and since I found out about my cousin's death. And now it was time to go back to Atlanta. Exhaustion had taken over body and it hurt to even move. No amount of coffee could surge me to life. No amount of hot showers could relax me.

The only thing I found joy in was my daughters' laughter. If it weren't for the bliss in their giggles, the sweetness in their voices and their cute faces, I would have laid in bed the rest of my stay in Virginia.

My husband was being icier than usual. It was like an Alaskan winter whenever we communicated. Frigid and brutal. He hadn't comforted me when my aunt died nor did he bother to comfort me when I told him about DeeDee. It was as if he didn't love me anymore. I knew that the attraction was lacking on his end, but I thought he cared enough about me to make sure that I was ok. I was wrong. We haven't spoken since I told him about DeeDee. What kind of husband does that?

"Are you ready to go to the airport?" My mother asked me when she tapped on the bathroom door. I was pulling a wig on my head because I didn't feel doing anything to my hair.

"Yea, I'm just about ready. Our bags are by the door," I replied.

"Ok, I'll start putting them in the trunk. Come on down soon, we don't want you to miss your flight," she added.

Since my mother made that comment about my weight, I had been walking on eggshells around her. I had eaten very little in her presence and I avoided conversation with her. She was far too critical of me. I needed support, not someone tearing me down. Food couldn't be my support system. My husband wasn't. The only thing I could do was keep my feelings bottled inside and that was forcing me into depression.

Moments later, I walked downstairs and retrieved the rest of our bags. Before going outside to the car, I pulled out two Twinkies and stuffed them in my face. I needed to sneak treats so that my daughters wouldn't ask for anything and so that my mother wouldn't say shit to me.

Once I was satiated, I head out of the front door. I sat in the front seat while the girls were buckled behind my mother and I. Finally, I was going back to Atlanta. On the way to the airport, I attempted to call my husband several times to ask him if he could come get us from the airport. Each time I received no response.

I knew that he was busy with the election but he needed to answer the phone when I called. We have children and it could have been a dire emergency. "Ugh," I grunted aloud.

"What is it?" my mother asked.

"Braxton won't pick up the phone. I need him to come get us from the airport. I have all of these bags and I need help with the girls," I replied.

"The man is trying to become mayor. Stop worrying him with frivolous things. Instead you need to worry about becoming a trophy wife. He needs to have a woman on his arm that he can be proud of." Her words pierced me like a syringe to the heart. Did she even hear herself? What does the way I look have to do with him helping us get home from the airport? I swear she was the most backwards thinking woman I knew.

I didn't even bother dignifying her comment with a response. Instead, I remained silent until we got to the airport.

"Goodbye my beautiful babies. You be good and don't give your parents a headache," my mother said hugging my daughters.

"We love you Grandma," they cheered before we walked away.

I took a deep breath in because I knew that this was going to be hectic. Getting through the airport with three children and three suitcases was no easy task. To get things moving along, I sat my youngest, Zoe in a stroller.

"Braxley, I need you to push Zoe for me," I directed. Excited to be mommy's little helper, she gripped the stroller. I then found a cart for all of our suitcases and placed them on top.

"Robyn, I need you to hold my hand, ok? Don't let go."

"Yes, mommy."

I needed to know where my babies were at all times. I never wanted them to veer too far away from me. You weren't going to see me on the evening news talking about, "I don't know where she went. She was just right here."

Together we made our way through the airport. Pushing the heavy cart and holding on to a fidgety fiver year old was cumbersome. But finally, we made it through the bag check, security check and front gate.

Walking down the tiny aisle always made me anxious. Because of my size I often bumped into passengers. "Excuse me. I'm sorry. Pardon me," had become my airplane aisle mantra. It made me so uncomfortable that I tried my best not to use the bathroom while the flight was in the air. I couldn't handle the humiliation. Most people didn't mind but there was always an asshole sucking their teeth or mumbling something about me needing to lose weight underneath their breath.

After getting situated on the plane, I was drained. I handed Robyn and Braxley iPads so that they could watch shows and play games. Zoe fell asleep with her little head leaning on my shoulder. And not before long I had fallen asleep too.

* * *

Hours later, we had arrived in the A.

"Thank God we're home!" Braxley shrieked. We were all tired from the trip.

"Yep, let's go get our bags," I replied.

"I have to go the bathroom," Zoe cried.

"Me too!" Braxley followed.

"Me three!" Robyn chimed in.

I sighed in frustration. When one wanted to do something, they all wanted it. Monkey see, Monkey do. I just wanted to get in the damn house.

Finally, we got off of the plane and I whisked the girls to the bathroom which is always a tough task. Luckily Braxley was old enough to use it properly but Zoe and Robyn needed help.

When we stepped to the sinks and washed our hands, I held up Zoe so that she could reach. I caught a glimpse of my reflection in the mirror and grimaced at the sight. My skin looked dry and gray as an elephant's ass. My eyes were the color of red wine and I had more luggage under them than bag check did at this airport. I needed rest terribly.

We left the bathroom and went to luggage pick-up. While waiting for the conveyor belt to bring us our baggage, I phoned Braxton once more. I couldn't believe he had the audacity to not call me back! He didn't text or anything while I was on that flight. He knew that we were coming back today. I shook my head when he didn't answer, yet again.

I struggled to retrieve our bags, racing around the conveyor belt to grab them. When I would fetch one bag, another would come down and I would have to rush to the other side to get it. The airport was crowded with people, so having to push between them to get my things was exhausting and embarrassing. I even caught a few teenagers staring, pointing and giggling when I had to hustle to get our luggage.

If Braxton had showed up to the airport he could have done this for me. I am going to have a serious talk with him when I get in the house because this ridiculous. As my husband he should be more supportive. I retrieved our things, placed them on a cart and finally ordered an Uber. What kind of man would leave his wife and three young daughters at the airport to fend for themselves? I deserved better than this.

* * *

"Home sweet home," my oldest daughter called out when we walked into our empty home. Years ago my husband and I bought a beautiful colonial style home in Virginia Highland. It was an affluent area that housed singers, actors, athletes, doctors and lawyers.

The girls ran upstairs to their play room while I dragged our luggage inside. Exhausted, I poured myself a glass of Chardonnay and settled onto my plush couch before kicking my shoes off.

"Hmmm," I moaned. It felt so good to be home finally relaxing. That was the most tiresome and emotional three days of my life. As soon as I put these girls to bed tonight, I planned on being knocked out.

I checked my phone to see if my husband had finally decided to call me back but he hadn't. Pissed, I tossed it to the side and turned on the television. I decided to watch re-runs of Martin while trying to relax.

"Mommy! Mommy! We're hungry," the girls whined when they ran down the stairs. It was as if my job was never done. I decided to hit up Domino's and order a pizza. There was no way in hell I was going to cook after the day I barely survived.

Less than hour later, the pizzas were here and we were chomping down on them. The girls ate two slices each while I had devoured an entire pie. Despite eating a pizza by myself, I wanted to eat more. Just as I reached for the third box of pizza my husband pulled up.

"I think daddy is home," Robyn announced when we saw a car pull in to the driveway.

I rolled my eyes. I was too tired to fuss at him but I was livid that he would not call me back. The girls loved their daddy though. They dropped their pizza slices and ran to the door waiting for him to walk in. I paid him dust. I wasn't getting off of the couch to say shit to him. I continued munching while watching Martin on TV One.

The doorknob turned and in he walked. "DADDY!" The girls sung as they rushed to his legs, reaching for hugs.

"Hey princesses. I've missed you so much!" He exclaimed, leaning down and kissing each of them on the cheek.

"Hmmp," I sassed. If he missed them so much why wasn't he at the airport when I needed him to pick us up. His election campaign could have taken a two-hour break.

"Tell me about your trip," he said to the girls as he pushed his way through their clutches. He walked into the living room and they followed him like ducklings after the goose. He sat in the recliner chair while they all tried their best to squeeze in his lap.

Do you think he even bothered to say anything to me? Nope. He looked at me grimaced, shaking his head before doting over the girls.

"I'm going to bed. Tuck them in," I announced as I gathered myself off of the couch.

"Wait a minute, I just came home to grab a suit. I have to head to the office tonight."

"Why?" I asked, raising my eyebrow.

"I have an interview very early in the morning with The Atlanta Post."

"And why can't you leave from the house?" I wondered.

"They want to interview me in office and do a photoshoot. It's extremely early and I'd rather not disturb your sleep," he said.

"You are full of it, Braxton. Girls, go upstairs and let me speak to your father," I said.

"But mommy..." Braxley whined.

"I said GO UPSTAIRS!"

Lips trembled, eyes watered and more moaning occurred before they got off of his lap and trampled up the stairs. I knew they were mad at me but I didn't care. I needed to talk to Braxton.

"Braxton, what is going on? Why can't you sleep at the house tonight? And why didn't you respond to any of messages?! Do you know what kind of day I had?!? I had to run around the airport with THREE children without any help. Do you know how much work it is? Do you know what it takes to travel with children!? I needed you to pick us up!" I fussed.

"Well at least you got a little bit of exercise," he chuckled.

"Excuse me?" I hissed.

"Calm the hell down. I'm just joking. Look, I'm sorry Cipriana. I got caught up at work. This election has me going crazy. You know I have this fundraising gala coming up soon and I'm working on planning that. And tomorrow I have this interview at 7:00am in the office. Baby, we live almost an hour from the office and I don't want to fight traffic in the morning. That's why I need to sleep there tonight."

I took a deep breath, trying to compose my fire. I understood where he was coming from. I just hated that he couldn't do more than one thing at a time.

"You have a family too and we need you here."

"Don't you think I know that? I'm doing this all for you and the girls so that we can have a better life. You have to let me work and let me make it up to you. I'll give you a break and take the girls all weekend long. It'll be a daddy and daughters weekend out," he said.

"Please. I need a break. I'm tired. In fact, I have to get Robyn and Braxley up in the morning for school," I said. The girls went to private elementary school while Zoe went to one of the most expensive daycares.

"I know. I got you," he said as he began to walk away. I was amazed. I had been gone almost a week and he hadn't given me a hug or a kiss. But if he could fulfill his end of the bargain this weekend, I'll take it.

We had made it to our bedroom. I hadn't been in here since I got in from Virginia. It was exactly as I had left it; bed made, dressers dusted, mirrors clean and no clothes in sight. When it came at keeping house, I was damn good wife.

"You mentioned a fundraiser gala? When is it?" I asked, as I followed him up the stairs.

"In two months."

"Why didn't you tell me earlier? I could help you plan it."

"Ugh," he grunted.

"What?" I was confused as to why he made that weird sound.

"I didn't know how to tell you this, but if you're going to help me with anything concerning this campaign you need to present yourself better," he confessed.

"What do you mean present myself better?" My face twisted in disarray. What the hell was he getting at?

"Cipriana, if you're going to be the first lady of Atlanta, you're going to need to lose weight. Fix yourself up. Get your hair did. People are talking and they are saying you're going to hurt my chances at winning."

Ever single word that fired out of his mouth burned into my spirit. It was worst than the shit that my mother said. Unable to contain my tears, they flooded my cheeks, further cementing my embarrassment. I was doing the best that I could but I guess I could do better. If my husband needed to me to lose weight, fine. I could do that.

"I'm sorry that it came out that way," he attempted to apologize but by now he was rummaging through his suits in the closet. That apology wasn't the least bit sincere.

"It's ok," I replied. "I'm going to go tuck the girls in." I left the room and dried my tears before putting my babies to sleep. Once I drop the girls of at school in the morning, I vowed to go to the gym. I needed to lose weight fast. At this point I would do anything to save this marriage.

Chapter 8

Aria

"Bae, this week I want these diamond encrusted sterling silver hoops from Tiffany's. I also need those new Giuseppe boots. And babe, are we going to Monaco this year? You did promise we could take a vacation soon," I requested while having my nails done.

It was spa night in our house. Months ago I was able to convince Czar to have a manicurist, esthetician and massage therapist come to the house at least once a week to hook us up. I tugged on his guilt like a newborn to the nipple making sure I got every drop of what I wanted.

"No, no and maybe on the vacation but it won't be to Monaco," he replied. Frustration crinkled the lines of his forehead while Mimi massaged the kinks in his shoulders.

"What do you mean *no*? It's what I want…"

"Aria, chill out. You already have earrings like that."

"Yea but they aren't silver and they're about two centimeters smaller. I want the bigger ones."

"For what? That's ridiculous. I said no. And those boots? Aria you have thousands of boots that you've only wore once. Go look in your closet and put on a pair you haven't worn this year," he replied.

"Excuse you? What the hell has gotten into you?" I asked while fidgeting.

"Miss Brass stop moving or your nails will mess up," Alana the nail tech chided.

"You are asking for shit you don't need. And I already told you I have to start making some changes around here. I'm pulling out of the game and focusing on my businesses. And to open more clubs and possibly buy more property, I'm going to need to budget better. That means no more clothes and jewelry. Shit, you damn near got a jewelry store in your closet," he growled before standing up. He tossed Mimi's hands off of his shoulders and walked away.

"You owe me!" I blasted.

"Stop doing that Aria. You know I love you! You know how much it hurts me to see you like this. But baby I've given you the whole world. I've given you everything you could ask for already. None of this material shit is going to make you walk again. And as for me owing you? You are right. I owe you a safe and honest life. I can't do that by hustlin'. If you get shot again, you could die. I can't lose you," he pressed. His pacific blue ocean eyes, pierced into me and I could see that he was sincere. But I didn't care. I wanted what I wanted.

"We'll see what my father says..." I muttered.

"What did you say to me? Are you threatening me? I don't care. Tell your father. Tell him everything I just said to you too. Tell him about how I'm trying to protect you and you don't want protection. Tell him how spoiled and greedy you are. I don't give a shit. And all of this spa shit? This is the last day for it. You're going to be doing your nails your damn self," he barked before marching off.

"Where are you going?" I yelled.

"I need to take a drive. I'm going to Sweet Suite to handle business. While I'm gone, I need you to think about that threat you just made. What the fuck is your father going to do to me from inside of prison any damn way? Get your head right, Aria." Before I knew it he had snatched his keys and headed out of the house.

If he thinks my father has no power from inside his cell block, he had another thing coming. And as of right now, I don't need my father to do anything. I had a little power on my own. If my husband no longer wanted to provide and give me what I wanted, I had just the boss to replace him, Nokio.

Chapter 9

Apryl

I had been at the hospital day and night praying for him, waiting for him to wake up. There had been some good news; the swelling had gone down and now he lay in a coma. We just had to wait for him to wake up.

I hadn't been back to work in almost two weeks since I had been at the hospital at his aide. Human resources called me the other day to tell me that I had no more leave left and that I wouldn't be getting paid for any more days that I needed to take off.

I couldn't afford to not work, so I decided to go back to the office today. As soon as I get off my shift, I plan on heading back to the hospital to be by Kazman's bedside. Walking into the precinct was both nerve wrecking and relieving. I was scared about the mountain of work that I had to do but also happy to be back. Being at work would give me a break from worrying about Kazman and would give me a chance to make money so that I could pay my debts.

"Hey Apryl, welcome back. Any news on Kaz?" Andre, one of my co-workers asked. He and Kaz used to be partners before Kaz quit.

"The swelling has gone down. We're just waiting on him to wake up," I smiled.

"That's good to hear. Where was he when he got hit?"

"He was in Midtown. They still haven't' found his car though."

"No, that's not true," I heard Nichelle interject.

"What do you mean?"

"They just found his car. It's in impound. I can have it towed to your house."

"Thank you so much! Where did they impound it from?" I asked.

"They said it was on Piedmont Avenue not too far from where he was hit."

I thanked her for letting me know but I still thought it was odd the car had been impounded. Was it parked illegally? Whatever the reason was, I was happy that it would be brought back to me without me having to pay a fee.

"Apryl can I talk to you for a second privately," Nichelle asked.

"Sure," I replied following her into her office. "What's going on?"

"I wanted to give you a bit of good news."

"What is it?"

"You aced your undercover detective exam. The psyc evaluation went well too. You are ready to go undercover girl!" She exclaimed.

"Oh my god! That's the best news I've heard in days." My smile spread from ear to ear.

"There are a few assignments that we eagerly need cover for. One of them hits close to home for you. I'm not sure if you're going to be up for it." Her voice lagged with apprehension. She sat down into her office chair, a torn clothed seat that looked like the department picked up in a crack house raid. I knew that budgets were tight but she needed a new chair now.

"What is it? I need to work right now. I need to get my mind off of Kaz or I'll go crazy."

"Let me preface this by being transparent. You know that I look forward to being the first female police commissioner of Atlanta."

"Right. You know I support you."

"And that means I have to solve tough cases. Cases that most men can't even crack. If I can get a few headlines under my belt as lieutenant whoever is the next mayor will make me commissioner," she explained.

"Uh huh…"

"With that being said, I want to crack the trafficking ring in Downtown Atlanta and I think we start by infiltrating the Sweet Suite; the night club DeeDee died in. Over the last few years we've had our eyes on the owner, Czar Brass. Last year we arrested a woman who was stripping there but she was also being used as a mule.

"So you need someone to go undercover at the strip club and see if someone approaches me to be a mule?"

"Yes. I need you to find out if someone is dealing out of the club. I need you to tell me who and how they transport drugs so that we can catch these guys. Are you up for that?"

"Honestly, hell yeah. I need this Nichelle. I have to throw myself into my work and it would make me so happy if I can find out who is behind my cousin's death," I replied.

"Ok. I'll have Andre be your point of contact. Let me call him in so that I can brief him and we can devise a plan." She stood up from her chair and brought Andre into the room.

A part of me felt as if I should take it easy and just work at the desk but I needed to be in the throes of action. Besides, if I did well they would promote me. And if I impressed Nichelle enough I could be working for her in the police commissioner's office.

Andre walked in and sat in the seat next to me. I've always thought Andre was a cutie. He was about 5'11, copper tone skin, chocolate eyes and his hair was reddish brown. He had freckles specked throughout his face which I thought was adorable. He had been a good family friend to Kazman and I over the years. I knew that working with him would be smooth.

After Nichelle briefed Andre about the new assignment we headed out to lunch. My tastebuds were salivating for some Chick-Fil-A. I couldn't get enough of that Polynesian sauce drenched over a deluxe chicken sandwich. And throw in the frosted lemonade and those waffle fries, I would be in heaven.

"Are you sure you want to work undercover as a stripper? That's going to be crazy. You're gonna have to shake your ass and be half naked…"

"Ha! I'm not worried about it. Whatever it takes to get my cousin justice and possibly become Nichelle's righthand woman when she's the commissioner."

"I guess. But what about what Kaz will say about you working in a strip club?"

"Kaz knows that I want be an undercover cop. He knows that I'll be in compromising situations sometimes."

"I guess. But if you were my woman, there is no way in hell I would approve of you stripping even if its for undercover work."

"And that's why I'm not your woman," I quipped before hopping out of his car and walking in to Chik-Fil-A. When we pulled up, the drive-through line was wrapped around the corner. Niggas love chicken. I just don't understand why they can't park the car and go inside the empty restaurant. It takes way less time.

After we ate, we went back to the office to chat about our plan to infiltrate Sweet Suite. I would start sometime next week. Apparently, they were auditioning for new dancers. Of course, I would have to brush up on my twerking skills and buy some platform stilettos and g-strings. I think had this in the bag, though.

* * *

Hours after work, I headed home so that I could receive Kazman's car. I hoped that they wouldn't take long to tow it to our apartment complex because I wanted to be at his bedside this evening. As soon as I began to walk into the house, the tow truck pulled up with Kazman's Honda Accord.

"Thank God," I whispered to myself.

I rushed outside to get the keys from the driver while he released the car into a parking space.

"Here you go ma'am," he said handing over the keys to me and a clipboard with the receipt to sign. With the keys in my hand I returned to my home but not before I heard another car scurry around the corner.

Like a bat out of hell, the car came flying around the corner almost crashing into me. Immediately it stopped right before it turned me into road kill.

"What the fuck?!" I shouted but as soon as the words left my mouth, it became clear why they were driving that way.

It was the loan shark coming to collect on a payment. Since the whole ordeal with my husband I hadn't been able to pay him.

"Long time no see," he said when he got out of the car and started towards me.

"Eli, I've been meaning to get back to you," I responded. It was amazing to me how this man had so much money but had the audacity to dress the way that he did. It was if he hopped in a time machine that took him shopping at Woolworth.

"Well that's odd, Apryl, since I've been hitting you up. Listen, you are a beautiful girl and I would hate to see your husband lose you."

"I need more time, Eli. Please give me another two weeks." I hadn't paid Eli anything since I last hit up Nino for cash because he didn't give me enough.

"Right now, I can promise you this," I continued as I twisted my wedding and engagement rings off of my fingers. Those rings were a symbolism of my love for my husband but symbolism wasn't going to keep us together. Sacrifices needed to be made. I was going to have to tell him the rings were stolen or lost.

"Not bad, these will do for now. I'll get them appraised then I'll let you know what you owe me," he spat.

"Can I buy them back from you when I get the cash."

"We'll see," he said before sinisterly winking at me and hopping back in his car.

A sigh rushed from my lips as I watched him close the car door and pull away. I was doing all of this for my husband and damn it, he better had survived. As of now, I needed to hit up Nino. The last time he paid me it wasn't nearly enough. And now that I have to take care of Kaz's hospital bills I really needed the cash.

Chapter 10

Mayeka

A clear blue sky hang over my head, while the sun beamed on my back. Their was no wind whipping around so I felt like it was the perfect day to take a walk around the community with BJ. I pushed him in his Mimi Xari, a stroller that cost over $1500. I loved how my boo Braxton spoils us.

He even moved me out of Bankhead into Buckhead. The apartment that he rented for me was much bigger than any home I had ever lived in. Braxton did a good job of taking care of us. He furnished my entire apartment by buying me top of the line furniture from West Elm and Z Gallerie. Outside of paying my rent and my bills he gives me money every week for food, clothes and whatever else I wanted.

I just wished we could spend more time together. Now that his fat ass wife was back in town he had been spending less time with me. He still comes through almost every day but he cuts our us-time short. That's ok, because soon he will be mine.

After taking a few strolls around the neighborhood, I decided it was time to put BJ down for a nap. I was exhausted and needed a break. It was a lovely day but it was time to unwind. Pushing him back up the street, I headed back to my apartment.

"Let me help you with that, Honey Bunz…" I heard a voice say as I carried BJ and the stroller up the stairs. Who in the hell was calling me by my stripper name in broad daylight?!

When I turned to see who it was, I was disgusted to find that it was Eli; the simp that used to pay me stacks to shake my cheeks in his face.

"What the hell are you doing here?" I gasped.

"I followed you. I used to follow you back home every night to make sure you got in safely. But then you moved when you got pregnant. But that night you were at the club, it gave me another chance to follow you home. I just needed to make sure you got in without any problems," he said in a creepy voice.

He looked even more disgusting in the daylight. His skin was oily, leaving these bumps all over his face. His hair was scraggly and it looked like he never learned how to shave. This nigga looked like a bag of scabs. I wanted to throw that luxurious stroller at his head and run the hell in the house.

"What do you mean you followed me?! If you don't get out of here I'm going to call the police!" I yelled.

"No don't do that. You don't want to hurt my feelings again. That night when I was trying to talk to you at the club, you really broke my heart when you ignored me. But then I saw you leave the club, and I could tell you were drunk. You weren't intentionally mean to me. You were just drunk, baby," he said as he stepped closer.

"What the hell are you talking about. I swear to god, Eli get out of here!"

"Maybe you are drunk now? I know you had to be when you hit that man. You were so drunk that you didn't realize that you had hit him. That's why you drove away, right?"

"You saw me hit him?"

"Yes and I didn't tell the police because I knew my precious Honey Bunz didn't mean it. Just like you don't mean to hurt my feelings. And if you want me to keep your little secret to myself, I suggest you be nice to me."

My heart raced as I listened to him sleazily and underhandedly blackmail me. I'm guessing BJ could feel me become filled with angst because he began to cry loudly.

"Shhh shhh baby. It's ok."

"He's such a cutie," Eli complimented reaching out to stroke my child.

"Don't you touch him!" I growled, snatching Braxton away.

"Sorry. He should get to know me first since I'm going to be around a lot."

"He will never get to know you."

"He will if you don't want to go to jail for a hit and run. How about we discuss it over dinner Sunday night?" he suggested.

"Fine. Just please leave, I have to get him in the house," I replied, saying whatever I could to get him off my stairs. BJ continued to cry as I watched Eli walk away.

All of this time, I thought I had gotten away with hitting that man without any consequences. But this nigga had seen the whole thing. What kind of person does that? How could he stalk me?

Tears began to flow out of my eyes. It was as if BJ and I were in sync. Once I got in the house, I prepared him a bottle and settled on the couch. What the hell was I going to do about this nigga? I couldn't bare to go out on a date with him. Being seen out in public with him would make people stare. He was disgusting and I was a fly bitch.

Chapter 11

Cipriana

"Bye, baby." I kissed my Robyn and Braxley goodbye when I dropped them off at school. I had already taken Zoe to daycare before them. After pulling away I headed to a new gym, in Midtown which wasn't far from the kids schools. Today was the day I decided to take my health into my own hands.

When my husband told me that I needed to lose weight it was a serious wake up call. I couldn't lose him over stupid petty shit. I needed him home with me and those three girls because without him, I couldn't make it.

The sun beamed through my windshield, blinding my sight as I pulled into the parking lot. Sweat pellets were already forming on my eyebrow and I hadn't even ran or lifted a weight. Perhaps it was my nerves along with the bright sunshine that was causing me to heat up. Whatever it was, I refused to let it keep me from going into the gym.

Taking several deep breaths, I got out of the car and sashayed into the front door. I was wearing black leggings, a purple sports bra and a black t-shirt. On my feet I sported a pair of purple Pumas.

"I would like to sign up for a membership," I stated confidently to the front desk woman.

Her face broadened into a welcoming a smile before responding, "Sure. Let me give you a tour. We are giving free trials right now, would you like to start there?"

"No. I need to go ahead and pay. I know if I pay for it, I'm more likely to use it," I replied.

"Okay. I can get you set up."

I went through the process of signing up for the gym and she gave me a tour. Afterwards I decided to take a stab at working out. I had purchased a workout plan from a fitness instructor I followed on IG.

The first work out was squats, something I had never done before. I went near the squat machine and attempted to figure out how to use the damn thing. Frustration brewed within me as I pulled out my phone googling how to do the exercise.

"Excuse me shawty, you need some help?" I heard a voice say from behind me. His voice had bass with a touch of raspiness. It was the sexiest voice I had heard in a long time. Before I could answer he stepped even closer this time wafting the scent of his cologne around me.

"I don't want you to hurt yourself," he continued.

When I looked up to see who it was, my eyes grew big and I became a bundle of nerves. He was a fine as nigga with dark skin, a thick beard, and a strong jaw. Across his teeth was a grill that looked more luxurious than most bitches wedding and engagement rings. His hair was cut low and he had more waves than the Pacific Ocean.

"Yea, I'm new to this," I answered him while biting my bottom lip.

"It's all good. I can show you how to do it. My name is Javi by the way. What's yours?" he asked me while reaching out his hand.

"Cip…Cipriana," I stuttered. *Get it together girl!*

"That's a pretty name, I ain't never heard no shit like that before."

"Thank you," I smiled.

"You got a beautiful smile too."

"Thanks. Are you a personal trainer?"

"Not officially but I know what I'm doing. This is my gym and I don't want you coming in my spot hurting yourself them trying to sue me" he chuckled.

I sucked my teeth and flashed a sheepish grin. He was cute and managed to make me giggle. When I glanced at his muscular body I could see that he definitely wasn't lying. His muscles bulged out of his tank top and they were decorated with tattoos. He had an entire sleeve of tats, looking every bit of scrumptious. He was so different than my husband and I couldn't believe that I was attracted to him.

"So do you want me to help you?" he asked me again. I must have drifted off in to la-la land.

"Um, sure."

"What are you working on?"

"This." I handed him my work out plan that I purchased. I watched as he scrolled it, nodding his head in approval. My eyes studied his every subtle movement; from the way that his jaw clinched, to his muscles flexing. He was a work of pure art. It was if God had carved a mini god out of dark chocolate.

"Aight, so baby girl this may be a little advanced for you. You need someone to walk you through the entire process. I can do that for you. After a couple of weeks of working with me, then you can start this plan," he stated before handing my phone back to me.

"How much do you charge?" I asked.

"I'm not going to charge you. I told you, I don't do this professionally. Whenever I see a beautiful woman like yourself working on their fitness, it makes me proud. I just want to help you reach your goals," he answered, while smirking. *Gawdamn he was fine.*

"And we can start today?"

"Yep. We can meet every other day for the next couple of weeks. Cool?"

"Thank you so much."

"Yea. Lemme get your contact info so that I can call or text you if something changes," he said.

I handed him my phone again.

"Oh you're married? Why your husband ain't in here with you?" he asked when he noticed the platinum band around my ring finger.

"He's so busy…"

"Nigga should be in here encouraging you. Even if he at work, he could come early in the morning or in the evening with you," Javi spat before returning my phone.

I shrugged it off, not knowing what to say in response. There was no way Braxton was going to ever come in here with me. It's as if he is embarrassed by me.

"Aight, let me test where you are in your fitness. First let's try a plank," he said.

He got down to the ground in a push up position. His shoulders and arms looked even more pronounced. I could envision them wrapping around me while he made love to me.

Oh my god. Get it together, Cipriana. You're married!

"Come down here with me," he commanded.

Doing as he said, I knelt into a plank position. But unlike his sturdy arms, my jiggly biceps and shoulders, could barely hold my body up.

"Ok nice, stay right there," he instructed. He stood up and hovered over me. My arms felt like twigs holding up a bridge and the fact that he was so close to me didn't help either. My nerves tensed and rattled under his aura.

"You gotta lift your hips up a little higher," he said as he slid his hands to my hips, raising them. His masculine touch drove me wild. Damn, am I pathetic? It's been so long since my husband has put his hands on my hips that I'm getting tingly from him touching me in plank.

He tugged at my hips once more and I just couldn't hold it any longer. I plopped out right there on the gym floor.

"Good job. You held that for about 30 seconds," he chuckled while helping me off of the floor.

Embarrassment washed over my face because I couldn't hold it longer than 30 seconds.

"That's a good thing. You will get better as time goes on," he encouraged.

"I hope so."

"I promise," he said before guiding me over to the treadmill. He had me run for a few minutes until I grew winded. After that he had me do a series of other tests. Most of which required him to lay his hands on me. *Whew.* If I wasn't married I would probably be asking him to come back home with me. But I had self-control. I would never cheat on Braxton. Besides, I was in the gym for him. I was here to make my marriage work.

"So I'll see you on Wednesday." Javi winked goodbye once we wrapped up. I smiled and waived as I got back into my car.

If I wasn't careful that man was going to be a problem.

Once I got home, I showered. I must admit it did feel good to exercise. By the time I got out of the shower, cleaned and prepped dinner it was time to pick my children up. I hurried up and got dressed so that I could retrieve little Zoe first.

* * *

"Good afternoon Ms. Nicks. I need to talk to you for a minute," the director of the daycare greeted me.

"Um ok. Is everything ok with Zoe? Did she get hurt? Is she in trouble?" Of course, I jumped to the worst conclusions.

"No it's nothing like that. I just wanted to talk to you about her tuition. Can you step into my office?"

"Um, sure," I replied, following her.

"I know this isn't normal of your family but your husband hasn't paid Zoe's tuition this month. Can we expect by tomorrow?" she asked, fixing her zebra print glasses.

"Wow, I had no clue. I will get back to you tomorrow," I announced.

"Please do. Everyone loves Zoe here, and we would hate to see her go."

Me too.

"I will speak to my husband tonight. I have to pick up our other two girls," I announced.

"Sure thing. Best of luck," she waived me goodbye.

Baffled, I picked Zoe up and placed her in the car seat before making my way to the other children's school. Why in the hell hadn't Braxton paid her daycare tuition? He is typically good about this kind of stuff. The campaign couldn't be that damn distracting.

Moments later I pulled up to Braxley and Robyn's school. Usually, they were waiting outside with their teacher but today no one was there.

"Shit," I grumbled.

"Uh oh," Zoe cooed and covered her mouth. She did that whenever I said a "bad" word.

"Sorry sweetie," I said before getting out of the car. I gathered her out of her seat and together we walked into the school.

"Hey Ms. Roberts…"

"I know you came in for Robyn and Braxley but the admissions office needs to speak with you."

The way that she spoke to me reminded me of the director of Zoe's daycare. Were these people going to tell me that this tuition hadn't been paid either?

"What's going on?" I asked, placing a squirmy Zoe on the ground.

"Robyn and Braxley's tuition hasn't been paid in two months. We've mailed correspondence regarding this matter but we haven't heard anything," she revealed.

"I'll talk to my husband," I replied. I was beyond irritated. There was no use in even discussing this with the school right now. The person I needed to talk to was Braxton who typically got home around 7:00pm.

"Please do, or they won't be able to come back next month," she replied.

I gritted my teeth and shook my head. What in the fuck was going on with Braxton? I gathered my children and placed them in the car. The entire time I kept asking myself over and over why would he jeopardize our children's education.

When we arrived in the house, I started cooking and helping the girls with their homework. By 5:00pm homework was done. By 6:00pm dinner was made. By 7:00pm dinner was eaten. By 8:00pm the girls were bathed. By 9:00pm I was reading them bedtime stories. And my husband still wasn't home.

Once the girls were sound asleep, I poured a glass of wine and relaxed on the couch, counting down until the time he walked in the door. How was he not home yet?

As I sipped my moscato my phone buzzed. Leaping from the couch, I grabbed it thinking it was going to be Braxton. But to my pleasant surprise it was a text message Javi from the gym.

Javi: What up Shawty, be sure to drink a lot of water and eat healthy. Also take a cold bath if you're sore from the work out. See you Wednesday.

For some reason reading his text message drew a smile to my face. That man had a way of affecting me through a harmless text message. Grinning ear to ear, I responded to his message by telling him "thank you." As soon as I hit send, the front door opened and in walked Braxton.

"We need to talk," I announced when he closed the door behind him.

"Damn, CiCi, I just got in the fuckin' house. Can I at least take my jacket off," he barked.

"Why are you just getting in the house anyway? You were off of work hours ago?!"

"How many times do I have to tell you this?! It is election season and I have much more work to put in. I've told you that countless times. Do you have fat in your fucking ears?!"

"Hold up, Braxton. Don't you talk to me like that! First of all, our daughters are upstairs sleeping! Second of all, I am your wife. How could you speak to me that way?!" I could feel the waterworks about to run down my face. My bottom lip trembled while my voice cracked.

"I wouldn't have to say that shit to you if you would listen the first time! Damn, I can't even come in here and relax."

"Why didn't you pay the girls' tuition?" I asked, changing the subject. Fuck his relaxation. I haven't relaxed since I woke up this morning.

"Shit. I meant to tell you. I've just been busy..."

'Tell me what?!" I thrashed.

"Tell you that I'm pulling them out of private school. Just for a couple of years," he said. He walked closer into the house and made his way into the kitchen. As soon as he got there he looked at the plate I prepared him on the stove; fried chicken, string beans, candied yams and honey butter rolls.

"Ugh chicken again??" He complained.

This man had the nerve. I slaved over that stove with hot grease popping in my eye and he has the audacity to turn his nose up at it.

Ignoring his snide comment, I asked once more, "What happened to their tuition money?"

"Well, Cipriana if you must know, I'm pulling them out of private school because it looks better for my campaign. The people of Atlanta don't want to vote for someone who has their kids in private school. It says that I think I'm better than them. It says that I don't trust Atlanta's public school system. I need the people to believe in me and I need them to believe in the school system," he replied.

"Why wouldn't you tell me? You didn't even discuss it with me."

"It's my money," he stated flatly before reaching in the freezer and pulling out a T.V. dinner.

I shook my head at the disrespect. Braxton was transforming into a man I didn't recognize.

"It's our money. We are a team. We're married, remember?" I asked holding up my ring finger, flashing the band that was supposed to symbolize our unbreakable bond.

"You don't work. I do. Sure you made some money from selling your little books but you don't have a dime to your name. This cash is money I made. So if I want to pull the kids out of private school to further my career, thus ensuring you can continue to spend my money, so be it."

"What about Zoe? You didn't pay for her daycare," I replied while flaming tears fell from my eyes.

"You don't work. You can watch over her during the day," he replied.

"Why are you being like this to me."

"Do you want me to be mayor not?" he asked before walking away.

All I could do was break down and cry. He had become increasingly mean and now it was affecting our girls. I just didn't know what to make of this change in him. I hoped that me losing weight could help him treat me better. And maybe if he won the election things would change.

I left him in the kitchen to eat the microwavable meal while I went up to our bedroom to sleep. I closed my eyes and decided to fantasize about Javi. I knew a girl like me had no chance with a nigga like him, but it couldn't hurt to daydream, especially since there was no love coming from my husband.

Chapter 12

Aria

"What time did you say my husband is supposed to be meeting you here?" I asked Nokio, while he paced the floor. I knew that we didn't have time to fuck but damn I was craving his dick. I cared about Czar but I liked that Nokio had time for me. Czar was always working.

We were at the mansion in the living room, discussing a way to take over his empire. Near our gold fire place were to throne-like chairs. One for Czar and one for his queen. I sat in Czar's thrown while trying to figure out a way to dethrone him before he threw it all away.

Don't get me wrong, I love Czar, but I can't be with a semi-broke nigga. I refuse to struggle especially after what happened to me. If he was going to throw this empire away, then I was going to pick it back up.

"He said twenty minutes. I need you to tell me why I would even help you do this?" Nokio asked me. Nokio had been working with my husband for years but not as long as Javier who has known him since they were toddlers.

"Because you love me…" I licked my lips attempting to entice him. Nokio was fairly attractive. He stood at 6'0, no where near as tall as my husband, but taller than me. His skin was warm caramel complexion and his hair was in dreads. I knew that if I flirted hard enough I could convince. Don't ever discount a handicapped bitch. Besides he already knew how good this pussy was.

"That's a stretch," he laughed.

"Fuck you nigga. Let me make it plain for you. I know you're underpaid." I smirked. I pointed to the chair that sat beside me, the queen's thrown, directing him to sit down.

"How?" He asked.

It was clear that I was going to be the mastermind behind this. He was dense.

"Because I count the books. I have access to everything. Passwords, payments, finances, locations; you name it. I know everything. Have you ever wondered how Javi is ridin' around in a Lambo just like Czar but you're still pushing a '10 Accord?"

"You sayin' he pay Javi more than me?" Gosh this nigga was slow. How had he not figured this out from jump? I think the only person who wasn't getting paid more was Nino.

"Yes, that's exactly what I'm saying. Don't you want to get your bread up? Aren't you ready to be a boss like Czar?"

"Hell yea. I just don't know if I should go about it this way Aria…"

"Look around Nokio. This could all be yours. You're living in an apartment while Javi and my husband are both living in the lap of luxury. Let me help you get all of this," I said raising my arms wide.

"How?"

"First we need to get him in trouble with his connect. I was thinking we stage a robbery…"

"Only Javi and Czar know who the connect is…"

"I already told you I have access to everything. Do you see all of these boxes in here?" I said referring to all the shit we hadn't unpacked yet. I was supposed to be going through the files this week to organize the shit. Czar had been asking me repeatedly but I had been too caught up on Polyvore and eBay trying to get me some new vintage sandals for the summer.

"Aight, so you're going to find out who the plug is. And I'll get a squad for the robbery?" he asked.

"Ding! Ding! Ding! Once we do that, then we will go from there. Ok?"

"Sure…" We shook on the deal and just as our palms touched, Czar walked in through the door.

"Hey Czar," Nokio held out his hand to dap him up.

"Yo get the fuck out. Go back to the Sweet Suite and I'll meet you there. I gotta talk to my wife," he ordered. I could tell by the volatile sound in his voice that something wasn't right. Did he know about what Nokio and I were discussing or about us fucking? If so that meant that I would probably be murdered. Well, if he did he would have killed us on the spot.

"Damn man… calm down…" Nokio replied. See, this nigga didn't have too much sense.

"I said get the fuck out right now!" Czar growled but his eyes were steady burning into me.

"What's wrong with you?" I asked him, cocking my head to the side.

"What the fuck is this?!" He asked shoving a health insurance document in my face. It was a receipt of an abortion I had almost a year ago right before I was shot.

Immediately, my breath left my body and I felt as if I were going to pass out. There it was, staring in my face. It was one of my many dark secrets. Proof that I had an abortion last year.

"Baby let me explain…" I whimpered.

"Explain what? How you killed my baby when you knew I wanted kids? What the fuck? How could you do some shit like this and not tell me!?"

"How did you even find this?" I wondered as my stomach twisted in a bunch of tiny knots.

"Are you seriously asking me that right now?" He said shaking his head.

"I'm so sorry. Please…"

"Shut the fuck up Aria. Why did you do it? Huh? Can you tell me why you killed my seed? We been trying all this time! Is this why you can't get pregnant now? Shit, or are you on birth control again?!" He shouted a barrage of questions at me.

"No… I'm sorry Czar. I was scared. It was last year before the robbery. I just had this strange feeling something was going to happen. I knew that you were beefing with the East Side Boyz and I just didn't know what to do…"

"So you killed my child without telling me. What, you didn't think I could protect you and the baby?"

"WELL YOU COULDN'T! LOOK AT WHAT HAPPENED TO ME!" I spat, pointing at the wheelchair. Bingo. Every argument we had, I could always bring it back to the damn wheelchair.

His jaw clinched and he began to rub his head. He turned and walked away. With all his rage and disgust for me he smashed his fist into the wall leaving a large ragged gaping whole.

"See, that's why I didn't tell you. I had this feeling last year that I could be shot or the baby could be harmed. And I was. Look at me now, I'm a wheelchair for life! I'll never walk again. If I were pregnant when I was shot last year, I would have lost the baby any fucking way! I didn't do this to me! You did!" I screamed at him, making him grow angrier. I played his heart strings like a fiddle.

Am I evil for not feeling bad about this?

The truth is, I was cheating on him last year with the nigga that robbed me. The nigga got me pregnant after I repeatedly told him to pull out! When I became pregnant, I wasn't sure who's it was so I killed the damn thing.

"I gotta get out of here," he spat while turning away.

"Oh so you can come in here, huff and puff, make me feel like shit then walk away?!" I screamed from behind him. Placing my hand on my controller I spun towards him, following on his heels.

"Don't fucking follow me Aria. I need some time to think. I'm going back to the club. I'll see you tomorrow."

"Tomorrow? You not coming home?" I asked.

"Nah. I told you I need some time to think. I know that you not being able to walk is my fault but you could've told me about the baby. If you had told me you were afraid, you know I would have placed you in hiding. Instead, your ass kills my baby then ran off to party in Vegas like it wasn't anything," he replied, shaking his head.

True. I did fly out there to party and celebrate getting rid of that baby. It's my body, my choice.

"I think that's fucked up. But do you Czar. You always do this. You leave when you know I need you the most," I whined as he stepped out of the door, ignoring me.

As soon as I heard his car pull off, I took the elevator upstairs to the office so that I could go through those boxes and find out every bit of info on his business as I could. Now that he knows about the abortion, he was never going to forgive me. In fact he might even kill me. I had to get to him first.

Chapter 13

Apryl

Bright auburn wig. Check. Face full of make-up with contouring and highlighting. Check. Thotty outfit; ripped leggings, jeweled bra, 6-inch platforms. Check. My new look had me completely unrecognizable. When I viewed myself in the mirror I looked like I would win a *Thot of the Year* contest. But whatever gets the job done.

"Are you sure you're down for this?" Andre, my partner, asked me while looking me over. By the way his lips curled in disgust I could tell that I looked exactly how I should to get this gig, stripping at the Sweet Suite.

We gathered in my new apartment that the detective department rented out for me. Since I was going undercover deeply, I needed a whole new identity which included a new place, car, look and name. For my assignment I was changing my name to Jessica Mathers and my stripper name would be Cola Caine.

"Whatchu mean? I've come this far. There's no turning back now," I replied while putting the finishing touches on my lipstick. Puckering my lips together, to make sure that the matte pink color was distributed evenly, I turned to the side to see if my ass was sitting up right in those leggings.

"You can always say no, Apryl."

"If I say no the department will think I'm soft and I'll be on desk duty until I retire. I need this. I have to crack this case. Besides my little cousin died in that damn club. I owe it to her. She deserves justice," I protested. But the way that he shook his head let me know that it was falling on deaf ears.

"Your cousin brought this on herself. How many times have you warned her about the crowd she hung with? Even your husband had to sit down and warn her, yet she refused to listen."

"That's enough Andre. I have to leave anyway, my audition is at 6:00pm," I cut him off.

"Aight. I'll be here when you get back. Remember to be observant. I need you to tell me everything that you learn."

"Got it," I replied before picking up my purse, that held my new identity.

Leaving Andre in the dust, I rushed out to the '05 beat up Toyota Camry that was given to me for the job. As soon as I opened the dented door the stench of mildew wafted into my face. "Gross," I muttered as I climbed behind the wheel.

I sped away to the Sweet Suite, all the while listening to Drake's *Passionfruit* on the radio. During the drive, I thought about what dance moves I would do to ensure that they hired me. I had some experience on the pole since I used to take classes but that was a couple of years ago. It was a fun a hobby of mine that kept my body in shape but I had to quit so that we could save money. Paying for Kaz's tuition was more important. I had been meaning to buy my own pole so that I could practice at home. Maybe when this case is over.

* * *

Finally, I pulled into the parking lot of the club. From the outside it looked like an industrial warehouse; drab, black and boring. However when I walked in, I was astonished at how luxurious it looked. The walls were lined with mirrors and multi-tiered chandeliers hung from the ceilings. The floors were mahogany wood and the bars were made of crystal.

"Can I help you?" A tall dark skinned man asked me. I hadn't even noticed him sitting at one of the tables in the middle of the club.

"Yes, I scheduled an audition. I'm Cola Caine," I replied.

"Cool, I'm Javi, one of the managers. You'll be dancing for me and the owner Czar. He should be here any second," he replied. He walked over to me and shook my hand. He was very handsome and had that dirty south look most women would die for. His fronts gleamed in his mouth, a dazzling contrast to his cocoa skin. His beard was perfectly groomed and his tats were enticing.

"You ever danced before?" He asked me.

"Yeah, I used to dance in Memphis at the Star Lounge," I lied. In addition to the new home and car, I had a new life story. Andre and I spent days researching and drilling it into my head.

"Oh shit, I've been there a few times. I had family in Memphis. I ain't never seen you before," he stated.

"Maybe you missed me," I smirked.

"Maybe… You not my type anyway. Too little," he had the audacity say.

"Everything ain't for everybody."

"True. You from Memphis?"

"Nah, Richmond, VA, but I've had to travel around."

"Yeah, I feel you. Well, Czar should be here soon. In the meantime, can I make you a drink?" he offered.

"No thank you," I replied. I wasn't supposed to drink or do drugs undercover. But my nerves began to twitch letting me know that getting through this audition was going to be tough.

"Aight," he said before turning and walking away. He settled back in the chair and began to scroll through his phone.

Moments later the door opened and another man walked in.

"Yo, Nokio where is Czar?" Javi asked.

"He on his way. That nigga just kicked me out of his house. He said he had to talk to Aria about something. Nigga looked angry as hell," Nokio replied.

"Ahhh shit. When it comes that girl he gets hemmed up. It may be a while before he gets in here." Javi shook his head.

"Shawty, it's gon' be a while. Are you cool with waiting?" Javi asked me.

"That's fine," I answered. I sat at a booth towards the back of the club away from the two men and begin to wander through my phone as well. I really needed to get this audition over with so that I could go visit my husband tonight. This was the last time I would be able to see him for a while. Nichelle said it was best that I had minimum contact with my friends and family.

About a half hour later, other strippers rolled into the club to get ready for the night. Tapping my nails and playing in strands of hair of the cheap shitty wig, I let out a loud breath. I was bored as hell and ready to go. If Czar didn't come soon, I would miss visiting hours. I needed to see Kaz and kiss him on the cheek before I went all the way in.

"Damn nigga, where you been?" Javi shouted when Czar walked in.

As soon as this Adonis-looking man stepped through the doors, the energy in the room shifted. I swear it got hotter in here. My palms began to perspire while my heart thumped faster. He was beautiful; creamy light skin, jet black waves and a pair of cobalt ocean blue eyes that I could drown in.

"Had to handle some shit. Wassup," he marched over and shook up with Javi.

"Did you forget we had an audition today?"

"Shit. I did. Where she at?" He asked.

"Right there," Javi pointed to me. By now I had stood from the table and walked closer to the center of the club.

"You ready? I don't have much time," he spat rudely. His attitude took away from his fineness. In the end it didn't matter since I was married and apparently he was too.

"Actually, I been ready for the last hour," I quipped.

"Oh you a feisty one," he chuckled.

"Damn right. I know your time is important but so is mine."

A smirk widened across his face as he looked me up and down. "With all of that mouth you better be able to work a pole," he teased.

"You'll see..." I walked past him and climbed onto the stage.

"Can I get some music?" I asked since he and Javi were just standing there.

"Yea, I got you," Javi replied before walking away to the DJ booth.

Czar eased into one of the seats that sat in front of the stage. He whipped out his phone while I waited for Javi to play some music. The entire time, all I could do was stare at him.

This was the man that I was supposed to be investigating for drug trafficking, yet all I could think about was sitting on his dick and riding him. This was going to be tough but I had to keep my pussy in check. For one, I'm married. Two, he's married. And Three, this nigga is a criminal. He isn't worth going to jail or losing my husband for.

Finally, Javi turned on Future and Drake's *"Diamond Dancing"*.Despite my nerves, I got into it. I swiveled my hips like a figure 8, intoxicating both Czar and Javi. I could tell by the way their eyes studied me that I was doing a good job. Javi began to bob his head back and forth to the beat while, Czar's blue eyes lowered on me as if they were going to engulf my body. I wished they would.

As the bass line thumped throughout the club, I peeled off my layers of clothes, tossing them to the ground. Dancing in a black g-string with my titties out, I sashayed to the pole and began to twerk. My ass cheeks clapped back and forth.

Remembering what I learned in my pole dancing classes, I climbed the pole and popped my pussy in the air, surprising myself. Who knew I had the strength? Eventually, I slammed down into a split before crawling to the edge of the stage, the whole while Czar stared at me dumbstruck.

"That's enough," he replied before waiving his hand. Someone in the back turned off the music and his command.

"We need someone like you in here. Our best dancers have left over the last few months. You're sexy, got a crazy ass body, pretty and you can dance. Not to mention, that chocolate skin of yours is perfect," Czar complimented.

"When can I start?" I smiled while putting my clothes back on.

Apart of me felt weird for getting assed out naked in front men that weren't my husband, but I had convinced myself the ends justified the means.

"This weekend. Let's go talk logistics," he said as I climbed down from the stage.

"Good job," Javi praised as I walked by. I thanked him and continued to follow Czar, all the way to his office.

"So as you probably know this is a contractor gig. You only get paid the tips that get thrown at you. But every night you dance you must pay the house $350. That covers the DJ, security and the opportunity to get on one of the most coveted stages in Atlanta."

"Sounds good to me," I replied.

"What's your name again?"

"Jessica Mathers but my dancer name will be Cola Caine."

"I like that. Aight Ms. Cola. Welcome to the Sweet Suite. There are a few rules; no fighting, no drugs and no fucking in here. Contrary to what most people think, I don't allow that shit in here. Got it?"

"Got it," I replied as we both shook hands.

He had a tattoo of a name written across his knuckles however he snatched his hand away from me too soon. I didn't get a chance to read it.

"See you Saturday," I said before walking out.

Well that was easy but staying out of trouble won't be. That man was too damn fine. To wash his image out of my head, I decided to go visit my husband at the hospital one last time.

Chapter 14

Mayeka

"I'm coming over at 11:00pm," Eli's text message read causing me to grow extremely annoyed. I quickly stashed my phone away since it was 8:00pm and currently, Braxton was at my apartment, rocking our baby back and forth. He comes over every day after work to spend time with us. Sometimes he brings us money and other gifts. I wished that he could stay forever. But he keeps saying he can't leave that hog of a wife.

"Who was that?" he asked of the text message I just received.

"It was my sister Nyesha. She wants me to come visit her in Savannah but I can't do that with my car," I lied while poking my lip out. Well, it wasn't a full lie; she had asked me to come visit her.

"You know I can't get you a car right now," he replied.

"Why not? You see mine. That shit is about to die and go to car part heaven," I whined.

"You don't know how to take care of shit. Look at what you did to my car the night that you went to that hoe club," he charged.

"First of all you met me at that hoe club. Second of all, I told you someone else hit me."

"Give me a couple of days. I'll figure something out. Damn you're so spoiled," he said getting up and handing me BJ.

"You know you love it." I stood on the tips of my toes to give him a kiss.

"You're draining me, baby. After the car, I'm going to have cut back," he confessed.

"The hell you mean cut back? I can't work. Do you want me to go back to the club?!"

"Hell no. No I don't want you stripping. I can cover your bills and food but anything extra, nah. Maybe you should get a part time gig somewhere. When I become mayor you can quit. I just need to win the election and bam, I'll have access to the city's money."

"Fuck outta here. You said you would take care of me! Who's going to watch BJ while I work?"

"I'll figure that out. Just get a part-time gig for or something. You know I have three other kids. I had to take them all of out private school just so I could continue paying your rent."

"I don't give a shit. If I have to get a job, I'm going back to the club to shake my ass. I'm not going to sit in some office for $10 an hour when I can make 1k in a night!" I shouted.

"I don't have time for this shit. I have to go home to my wife. And if you ever want me to leave her and put you in that position, you will stay yo fast ass out of that damn club! End of discussion," he shouted before walking out and slamming the door.

The commotion caused BJ to stir and break out into tears. He screeched to the top of lungs which drove me insane.

"Shut up little boy," I hissed but it didn't help. He just continued to wail. I rocked him back and forth before settling on the couch. BJ balled his little fists up and began to scream even louder. I couldn't take it. I put him in the car seat, grabbed my phone and left the room.

Barricading myself in my bedroom, I turned on some the radio but I could still hear the little nigga screaming.

"If you would shut up and play your part, your father would be giving me what I want right now!" I shouted through the door.

That was the only real reason I went through with the pregnancy, so that Braxton would take care of me. BJ continued to cry but I didn't care. He could cry it out. Eventually, he would get tired and fall asleep. Sure, I loved my son but I couldn't listen to him scream all night.

I opened my phone to see if I had any notifications, lo and behold I did. Taunting me, there was a message from Eli. When I opened it, it read: Are you ignoring me? If you do I'll make sure the cops won't ignore you.

"Fuck!" I muttered.

I texted him back.

Me: You can't come over, I have no one to watch BJ.

Eli: I don't give a shit. I'm coming through. Make sure you wash that pussy for me.

"Ugh!" I groaned before throwing my phone to the side. If I didn't give him what he wanted then I could possibly go to jail. Why did that random nigga have to be walking in the middle of the street while I was driving home that night.

I left out of my room to check on Bj who, as I suspected, passed out from crying. I gently picked him up and placed him in his crib. I decided to get ready for this disgusting Urkle sleaze ball ass nigga by taking a shower and putting on some sexy lingerie.

Hours later he had arrived dressed like Forest Gump in a pair of khakis and a checkered button up. Where in the hell does he even find this shit?

"Oooh you look good," he complimented when I opened the door. I wore a lavender panty and bra set with a matching robe that had feathers around the collar and at the wrists.

"Thanks."

He slithered in my apartment without me inviting him in. I closed the door and watched him maneuver about, surveying my home. His eyes darted from the white fur rug to the light blue couches to the artwork on the walls.

"It's nice to see my money did you well," he said while tracing his fingers over one of the crystal lamps that rested on top of my end table.

"No... My son's father bought this," I replied while smirking. Sure, Eli was a good tipper back when I used to dance but most of his money went to my fabulous shoe collection, trips to Miami and Vegas and helping my sister out. Everything in this house was courtesy of Braxton.

"You know that kinda hurt me when you had a baby by another man. I thought we had something special." He slinked towards me, his eyes looking as if he were going to devour me. My skin bumped up as if there a thousand tiny spiders crawling on me.

"Well you were a customer…"

"So…?"

"Look, what do you want from me? Because I'd rather not talk about my son's father," I replied.

"I want the thing I've been lusting for. For the last few years Ms. Honey Bunz, you've been teasing me with those sexy lap dances," he replied while sliding his paws to my waist. My stomach whirled as if it were being placed through a meat grinder. If I had eaten earlier I would have thrown up on his face. I wish I had. Then there would be no way he would want to fuck.

"I was doing a service. You paid me to dance."

"Well it seems as if I did you a service. I was giving you money to shake your ass and now I want you to suck my dick. Repay me for not telling the cops that you ran that man down."

"That's it? You just want a blow job?" I asked. If it was just this time, I could live with that. If he wanted to fuck just for tonight, that would be fine. I would do anything to keep my ass out of jail.

"No, I want you to fuck me whenever I ask, until I get bored with you."

"Hell no! I have a boyfriend," I shouted.

"I'm not the person you want to say no to. Would you like to spend time in prison not being able to see your so-called boyfriend?" He sneered.

Biting down on my bottom lip, I shook my head.

"Ok then. Give me a show. I want a dance, I want you to suck my dick and then I want you to ride me like you love it."

"Let me just turn on some music," I replied before walking away. I switched over to my iPhone and turned on Ciara's Promise. When I returned to Eli, I took him by his hand and guided him towards the navy blue love seat that sat adjacent from the powder blue couch.

Once he eased into the chair, I bent over and shook my ass in his face and began to twerk. Left cheek. Right cheek. My ass bounced back and forth like a ping pong tournament.

"Oooh wee," he moaned as I placed my hand on my knees and began to swivel my ass in circles. I turned around and looked at him and I could see he was in ecstasy. Ugh. I hated this nigga.

He reached his hands to my hips and pulled me close so that I sat on his lap. I began to give him a lap dance like I used to do back at the club. Cocking my head back, I rested it on his shoulder before I nibbled on his ear.

"Hmmmm, Honey.." he moaned. I had never done that before. By now his hands were creeping in between my thighs, rubbing on my panties. Closing my eyes, I imagined it was Braxton touching me. That was the only way that I was going to be able to go through with this.

"You got a fat pussy. I've always wanted to rub it," he whispered in my ear. I must admit his breath smelled of winter mint. Thank God it didn't stink. However, fresh breath can't make up for the fact that this man was assed out ugly.

"Mhmmm," I forced out a moan before wiggling out of his lap and making my way to my knees.

"Damn, you don't know how long I been waiting to get you in this position," he spoke while I looked up at him.

"Well here I am," I breathed. I unbuckled his brown leather belt, courtesy of Grandpa's Fashions. And then pulled his khakis and boxers down, unveiling his dick. It wasn't big but wasn't small either. He had a decent package. When I leaned into put my mouth on it, I sniffed to make sure he wasn't stank but it smelled like Dove soap. Thank god.

Wrapping my hands around his shaft, I puckered my lips and gave it a kiss.

"Oh shit!" he said.

Ugh this nigga hadn't even felt my whole mouth and he was reacting crazily. Eli placed his hand at the back of my head and forced me down onto his dick. I began to suck it like it as if my life depended on it, because it did. This nigga was such a simp. The way that he moaned and squirmed was ridiculous. He reminded me of Blankman when a woman kissed him.

Without me trying hard, he ejaculated in my mouth. It was less than five minutes. Making him cum quickly was definitely a boost to my ego.

"Oh my God Honey, that was so good," he stated.

"I know." I rolled my eyes.

"Now sit on my dick," he ordered.

"Fine," I said. I spat on my fingers and rubbed my pussy to get juicy. There was nothing about him that would make me get wet. Finally, I lowered my sugar walls on to his dick. I squeezed really tight which caused him to moan even louder.

"Get on the floor," he demanded. While he was still inside of me, we made our way to the floor where he began to bang into me like a jackhammer. It was the worst feeling. It was a huge contrast from the way that Braxton sexed me.

I lowered my head down into the carpet while he smashed into me carelessly. Just as he got into it, BJ began screaming to top of his lungs.

"Stop, get off of me I have to check on my son," I announced.

"Not until I'm done!" he barked while grabbing the back of my neck and forcing me back down to the ground. BJ's cries grew louder and louder by the second.

"Please let me up!" I whined but he didn't. He continued pressing his dick into me while my son cried in the background. How could someone do something this heinous? On top of this motherfucker being hideous he was heartless. Well, I guess, I'm no better. I let BJ cry it out earlier.

"Take this dick, bitch!" He grunted while laying on top of me while my face rubbed against the carpet. I tried to fight him off, but he had a tight grip on holding me down. BJ wailed as if someone was hurting him. His howls were much louder than earlier.

For some reason it made me cry. Tears began to pour out of my eyes while Eli fucked me from the back. Before I knew it he was pulling his dick out and busting his nut over my ass. Just at that moment my son had stopped crying.

"Gawdamn you got some good pussy," Eli sighed before falling on to his back.

"Fuck you! My son could be hurt," I spat, struggling to get off of the ground. I rushed to his bedroom to check on him. I felt disgusting and cheap. Semen was smeared to my ass and tears were washing down my face.

When I finally approached BJ's crib, something seemed off. "Oh shit!" I shouted as I scooped him up.

He was barely breathing.

"Call 911!" I shouted to the living room for Eli.

"Nah you on your own. I gotta go!" he replied.

With BJ in my arms I rushed to the living room to find Eli escaping out of the front door. "Bastard!" I grumbled before reaching for my cell phone. I called 911 and placed BJ back down on the couch. I quickly got dressed and waited for them come.

I attempted to do CPR but I didn't know what the fuck I was doing. "Please don't let my baby die," I sobbed.

Chapter 15

Cipriana

The house was clean. Dinner was finished. And the he girls were bathed and tucked away in their beds. Now it was time for me to relax. As usual Braxton had gotten in late and was barely talking to me.

"I've been looking at schools to enroll our daughters in but then my mother offered to pay," I announced when he walked through the bedroom door. He began to undress, first by taking off his cufflinks then his shirt.

"It looks bad if a mayor's candidate has their kids in some expensive private schools. You just don't listen to me!" He shouted.

"Whatever," I replied before walking out of the bedroom, taking my phone with me. Every single conversation that we have lately involves him yelling at me for no damn good reason, and I was getting tired of it.

I went downstairs and sat on the couch and checked my text messages. I had a message from Javi.

Javi: Hey beautiful. Reminder, we have a session tomorrow at 10:00am.

I grinned at him calling me beautiful. Even if he wasn't being sincere, it was nice to hear it every once in a while. My husband never opened his mouth to say sweet things to me.

Tomorrow is going to be me and Javi's third session. When I met with him on Wednesday everything went well. There was certainly some chemistry between us two but I it could be all in my mind. He was so fine and in shape, I knew he couldn't have any interest in me.

I got up to grab me a bottle of water and drank it while watching television. Tomorrow was going to be a crazy day. I had to find the girls new school after Javi and I had our session, something I wasn't looking forward to.

Rather than go back upstairs and sleep with that iceberg of a husband, I fell asleep on the couch. But around midnight I heard trampling down the stairs.

"Shit!" I heard my husband shout waking me up out of my sleep.

"What is it?" I asked when I jumped out of the bed.

"There was a… um… a break in at my campaign headquarters. I have to go right away!" he said while shoving his feat into his shoes and heading towards the door.

"Call me as soon as you hear something," I groggily called out.

"Yea whatever," he spat before racing out of the door.

I shook my head. This man treats me like shit. If I could just lose the weight, maybe he would care about me again.

"You seemed a little off today when we worked out. Is everything ok?" Javi asked me once we were done exercising

"I have so much on my mind…"

"You want to talk about it? We can go get something to eat, my treat," he smiled.

"I don't know…"

"What's it gonna hurt? I know you're hungry."

"Why because I'm fat?" I thrashed.

"Um, no because you just worked out for an hour. And quit calling yourself fat. Your body is amazing."

"Oh yea? Tell that to my husband," I replied while shaking my head.

"Is that why you want to lose weight? For some nigga?"

"He ain't just any nigga. He's my husband. And right now we're going through some rough times…"

"Come on and talk to me over lunch," he suggested.

Unsure about doing so, I shook my head. Eating lunch with him was a slippery slope. I knew that going out to lunch with him would make me even more vulnerable to him. Right now I didn't need that.

"No. I can't. I have to look for new schools for my girls today," I replied.

"Aight shawty," he chuckled while simultaneously looking disappointed. He walked me out of the gym to the parking lot but just as I was walking out of the door, I noticed Sabrina, my husband's campaign manager.

"Hey Sabrina," I greeted.

"Hi Cipriana. Look at you! You got that workout glow. That's crazy. I'm glad you're feeling well so soon," she said causing my eyebrow to rise. I had no idea what she was referring to because I hadn't been ill.

"Thank you. Is everything ok? I heard about the break in," I said. Her eyebrows raised in confusion while she shook her head.

"My house wasn't broken into…"

"No, I'm talking about the campaign headquarters."

"Cipriana, I was just at the headquarters. There was no break in. Everything is smooth."

"What the hell?! Braxton left out late last night saying that someone broke into the headquarters. Why would he lie?" I wondered. Javi stood nearby listening in on the conversation. I had began to feel foolish. What in the hell was my husband hiding from me.

"Oh wow. No girl, there was no break in. He left headquarters yesterday around 5:00pm. I stayed behind contacting constituents…" she began to run on.

"Wait a minute, did you say that he left at 5:00?"

"Yep. That's what time he usually leaves."

"Was he at the headquarters this morning?" I asked her.

"Nope. It was just me and Julia, the assistant. He called this morning and told me you were very sick so he had to take you to emergency room last night. That's why when I saw you I was shocked considering you were just in the ER."

My skin flamed as I stood there listening to what she was saying. It was as if my entire world was crumbling down around me. Tears stung my eyes while my heart raced harder than it did while I was working out. Shaking my head, I cupped my mouth to keep myself from sobbing.

"Come one let's go get in my car and talk about this," Javi said.

"I'm so sorry Cipriana. I don't know why Braxton is lying to you. But I hope it works out," Sabrina comforted. Her eyes were filled with concern and mine were filled with shame. My husband was lying and I didn't know about what.

I shuddered as she walked away. Javi slid his arm across my shoulders and walked me away from the gym. Instantly I broke down into tears.

"After all these years, how could he lie to me? I'm doing everything to make him happy," I whimpered.

"It's ok," Javi said pulling me in for a hug. The strength of his arms felt comforting and protective but it wasn't enough to make me feel better about Braxton lying.

"He's cheating on me, isn't he?" I asked rhetorically but I knew it was true. Why else would he be coming home so late and leaving out in the middle of the night?

"Ask him. Make him tell you the truth. But to be honest Ci you already know what it is. That nigga don't value you. I can tell by the way you talk about him. He don't care about you and you deserve better. Despite the way that you feel about yourself you deserve to be with someone that respects you. From how you carry to yourself all the way to how beautiful you are, I know you are a good woman. It's too bad you're married to a fuck nigga that can't see that," he said while giving me another hug.

Javi had touched me more in the last five minutes than my husband had in five months. It felt good to be in his embrace but I really needed to leave so that I could get to the bottom of this.

"Thank you for your kind words. I have to go and figure out what the hell is going on," I announced.

"Listen, I'm here for you if you need to talk. Call me at any time. Aight?" He said to me before I opened the car door.

"I'll keep that in mind," I gave him a halfhearted smile. Javi leaned in and wiped my tears from my eyes.

"I mean it. Call me."

I nodded and hopped in my car. As soon as I did, I drove to my husband's office, which was separate from the campaign headquarters. While driving, I called him multiple times to no avail. What was he doing? The more I called, the faster I drove. I was livid and brokenhearted.

I knew without a doubt that he was cheating on me. I just wanted the details. When I got to his office, I spotted his car out front.

"Hey Ms. Nicks, I'm glad you're feeling better," one of his co-workers greeted me.

"Where is Braxton?"

"He's in his office," he replied. Without saying another word, I marched into his office, slamming the door behind me.

"What the hell Cipriana?" He asked while rushing to stand from behind his computer.

"Who is she?" My bottom lip trembled as the words spilled from my tongue.

"Who is who?"

"Don't play dumb with me? Who is the bitch that has you coming home late? The bitch that made you take money from your own children!

"Cipriana, you sound crazy right now. I don't know what bitch you are talking about." I could tell when he is lying. His eyes darted around the room and his fingers began to tap on the nearest surface.

"I just ran into Sabrina and she told me there was no break-in at the headquarters. Then she proceeded to ask me how I was doing because you told her that you had to take me to the emergency room last night."

His jaw clinched while he began to breath heavily. The look in his eyes told me he was caught in a lie.

"All these years Braxton I've been by your side. I've given up my career for you. Had three babies for you. Cook, clean. And this is how you repay me."

His lips spread into a devious grin. They parted and he let out a sinister chuckle before plopping back into his office chair.

"You're real funny Cipriana…"

"This is funny to you?"

"Yes. Here I am grinding my ass off to become mayor of this great city which will give you and our daughters a better life. I work hard so that you can sit at home and write those ridiculous stories you write, making hardly no money. And all you did was blew up like a balloon. So what if I step out from time to time to get me a little pussy. I come home to you and give my money to you. Now please leave so that I can get back to work."

My jaw dropped to the ground as his words penetrated my soul. I couldn't believe he confessed to cheating on me as if it meant nothing. The nerve of this nigga. My heart sank to the bottom of the ocean and I could hear ringing in my ears. Never in a million years would I think that he would be so callous and treat me like this.

"You are dismissed," he said. I must've been dumbstruck. I was certainly too paralyzed to move.

"You will regret this," I said before I walked away.

"Doubt it," he responded as I walked out of his office.

Chapter 16

Apryl

Tonight was my first evening where I'd be dancing at the Sweet Suite. But before I could go there I had to swing by Nino and get my money. My heart raced as I drove towards his block because I knew that it was risky. How in the hell was I undercover and extorting a drug dealer.

"Wassup Bacon," he spat when he walked towards my car.

"I don't have time for your shit today. Give me the cash."

"Here you go," he said as he shoved an envelope into my car. This particular envelope was much more heavy than the last one.

"I"ll be back next week."

"Yea yea," I hear you, he replied before I drove off towards the Sweet Suite. As soon as I pulled off, I received a call from Nichelle. In a bout of paranoia, I jumped and began to looking around. It was weird that she called me just as I left Nino, as if I were being watched.

"Hey Chelle," I greeted her.

"How's going? How do you feel?"

"I'm scared."

"You got this," Nichelle said through the phone.

"Yea, I know. I'm just concerned about Kazman."

"He's going to be fine. You just have to have faith in God," she replied.

"You're right. Well, wish me luck, I'm about to get of the car and walk in there. I'll report to Andre about everything that I noticed happening in the club when I get off."

"Ok girl," she said before hanging up.

With my belly tangled in knots, I walked into the club while wearing a sun dress. In my gym bag, were my stripper clothes. The auburn wig was secured tightly on my head and my make up was already done. My nerves were a wreck, worst than when I auditioned because this time I would be on a pole in front of a large crowd.

"Wassup new girl," Mike the bouncer greeted.

"Hey." I continued to walk to the back to the dressing room. On the way I passed Czar's office where I heard him speaking to Javi. Curiously, I leaned in closer to see if I could hear what they were speaking about. I wondered if they were bold enough to talk about dealing drugs right now.

"Czar, this bitch got a nigga weak right now. I aint even hit. There's something about her," Javi said.

"Nigga you wild. You've only known her a week. She married with kids and you talkin' bout you feelin' her?"

"You don't understand. She different from the rest of these thots."

"I don't trust your judgment. You the same nigga that used to smash Honey Bunz nasty ass. Now you on some married pussy," Czar teased.

"I'll admit Honey Bunz was a bad mistake. But this woman is different. We had lunch yesterday and I swear the conversation was better than any chick I had ever talked to. Her and her husband not doing well anyway. He a fuck boy that's cheating," Javi spat.

"Listen, just be careful," Czar said.

"Ahem," I heard someone clear their voice from behind me. It was Nokio with his frog looking ass.

"I was looking for the dressing room," I lied.

"Well it aint in Czar's office. It's that way," he quipped while pointing down the hall.

"Thanks," I said before walking away.

When I made it into the dressing room, I noticed three other chicks doing their make-up in front of the mirrors.

"You must be the new girl," one chick spat.

"Yeah, I'm Cola Caine," I replied.

"I'm Crown Vicky."

"I'm Caramel Chanel"

"And my name is Juicy J," they all introduced.

"You ever danced before," Chanel asked while smearing gold lipstick on.

"Yea, I used to dance at the Star Lounge in Memphis," I responded.

"When?" Chanel asked.

"About a year ago."

"Oh, I've been there to dance a few times as a special guest. I ain't never seen you before."

"You probably came on the days I had off," I lied.

"Maybe. You don't look like the typical stripper, especially not from the Star Lounge. Those bitches be busted," Chanel laughed while the other girls co-signed her.

I sat my bag down at one of the stations so that I could touch up my eyeliner and lipstick. Then I responded with, "I guess that was my appeal. I wasn't like their usual girls."

"I guess." Chanel shrugged it off.

"Do you know where I can score some blow here?" I asked the girls to test the waters. I needed to know per my investigation.

"Uh huh, Czar is strict about that. No drugs allowed up in here, especially after that last bitch died," Vicky spat, referring to my cousin.

I cringed at hearing her call her "that bitch."

"Excuse you, that's my seat," I heard a voice say. When I looked up into the mirror I could see that it was a tall thick chick talking to me. From the looks of it, I could tell that she was the thugged out bitch that probably thought she ran this place. Avoiding any trouble, I stood up from the seat and move out of the way to another bench.

"That's my seat too," she shouted.

This is what I get for moving in the first place. It was my fault for moving, letting these bitches know that they could run over me. This is the first lesson that you learn in the Academy; not to let these bitches see you back down. I made that mistake by moving once I won't make that mistake by doing it again.

Annoyed, I sighed and settled in even more. The broad stood behind me brooding over me while waiting for me to move. There was no way in hell I was going to move a second time. She was out of luck. To further cement my presence in the seat, I opened up my bag and sprawled my belongings out on the corner. All the while, I stared into the mirror, looking her big burly ass in the eye.

She cleared her throat violently, with the expectation that I would move. I rolled my eyes and reached for my cell phone and begin to scroll my social media sites. "I told you that that was my seat too, bitch! You need to move your ass now!"

Giggling under my breath, I stood up from the vanity and place my phone to the side. I walked up to her my face centimeters from hers, "I am not the one" I said as I stared her down.

Unexpectedly, she shoved me back which gave me my cue to pummel her ass. She shoved me into the vanity, banging my back against the table. It was all I needed to put this bitch in her place and let these other dancers not to try me again. As a trained detective, we've had to take years of combat. I knew how to fuck her up.

I smashed the heel of my palm in to her nose, jolting her head back. Blood gushed from her nostrils while her first instincts were to hold it.

"Oh shit!" Juicie J yelled out loud.

Disoriented, the huge chick came thrashing towards me but I stopped her by kneeing her in her abdomen. She buckled to the ground while hollering, "I'm going to kill that bitch!"

Just to make myself clear, I kicked her in her ribs to shut her ass up.

"What the fuck is going on in here?" Czar asked when he crashed into the dressing room.

"Bricks started it," Crown Vicky shouted out, backing me up. The fact that she was on my side shocked me but it also let me know that no one probably liked "Bricks"

"I don't give a fuck who started it. Damn, Cola Caine you just started and you're already starting shit. Go wait for me in my office!" He ordered.

Sucking my teeth I responded, "You heard Vicky, she started…"

"I said go to my office!" he repeated. The way that his eyes seared into my soul turned me on. For some unknown reason his wrath was sexy to me. A vein in his forehead pulsed, letting me know that he was serious. Following his orders, I left the room and went to his office.

"Ay Javi, help Bricks up. And Bricks you're fired. I'm tired of you starting shit in my establishment." I heard Czar say as I switched my ass to his office. My rose lipstick painted lips parted into a smirk when I heard him fire her. Hopefully, he didn't fire me too.

When I got to his office, my eyes searched around to see if there were any evidence of trafficking. I needed something, anything. The smallest clue could lead me to breaking this case. My eyes searched the entire office, but there was nothing unless it was hidden in the chestnut wood filing cabinets tucked in the corner.

Perhaps his desk drawers had something in there. It would be too hot if I decided to search through them right now.

Besides, the day after my cousin overdosed in the club they sent drug sniffing dogs in here to check of more drugs. They found nothing.

"Cola Caine," Czar called my name out when he stepped into the room. The way that it floated off my tongue made my pussy clench in desire. His cologne wafted to my nose before my eyes laid on him.

"Yes," I responded when he closed the door behind him.

"I am this close to sending your ass home. You haven't even danced here one night yet you're beating up my employees. What the fuck is up with that? At the audition, you seemed like you had some sense," he barked before sitting at his desk across from me.

"That bitch had it coming. And from the other girl's response she has always been a problem."

"Which is why I'm not going to let you go. Look, Cola..." he started to speak but stopped himself. He bit his bottom lip and ran his hands over his head, caressing his dark waves.

"Yes?" I responded.

"What are you trying to get out of this?" he asked me.

"I'm trying to make this money."

"There's more to it than that. There's something there when I look into your eyes. Do you have kids? Is it tuition? Do you owe someone? It just seems like you're well-spoken enough to be making money to do something else that would pay you good cash."

"Well, I am trying to get these dollars for tuition," I replied. It wasn't a complete lie. I had tuition to pay, it just wasn't mine. Thankfully, the department said that I could keep any tips I made while stripping undercover at the Sweet Suite as long as I included it in my taxes.

That was all fine and dandy, but I didn't want to be here that long. I wanted to be in and out. Shaking my ass for strangers was not what I considered fun.

"I figured it was something like that. Listen, I tell you what, I want you to bartend. And I'll match your tips. I've been wanting to start a scholarship fund but none of these bitches in here want to go to school. They just want to pop their pussies on the pole. They don't have long term goals."

My brows crinkled in confusion. I couldn't believe that he wanted to do something so thoughtful and selfless. What kind of drug dealer wants to send women to college. Knowing that he was willing to do that for me sent me on a guilt trip and I wasn't prepared to carry that baggage. For now on, I would feel guilty about taking his money while working here. This better transpire into a case or else I'm in the wrong.

"Cola? How does that sound?" he asked interrupting my thoughts. I licked my lips and nodded my head.

"Sounds good. When do you want me to start?"

"Tonight, You can shadow Kareem. He'll help you get acclimated."

'Thank you."

"By the way what are you going to go to school for?" he asked when I stood up to leave his office.

"Um, psychology," I replied.

"What school?" He pried. Ugh, why does he keep asking questions. With every lie that I told I felt worse and worse.

"Georgia State."

"Oh shit. My uncle works at admissions there. When you're ready to apply let me know. I might be able to help you get in."

"I'd appreciate that."

"No problem."

Feeling horrible, I walked out his office and went to the bar so that I could talk with Kareem. He was an older man with a potbelly, long gray dreadlocks and a scruffy beard to match. Despite being out of shape he was still attractive. He had a pair pretty chocolate eyes, a Crest smile and smooth pecan skin.

"Hi Kareem. I'm Z... Cola Caine," I corrected myself. Damn it. I had almost told him my real name.

"Nice to meet you Z'Cola Caine. I swear you strippers are a trip. Your names get crazier and crazier," he chuckled while wiping down the bar.

"No, it's just Cola Caine. I got a little tongue tied."

"That name ain't no better. And damn what happened to your knuckles?" He asked pointing to my bruised and bloodied hand. I had forgotten to wash my hands and bandage them after whooping Bricks ass.

"I just got into a little scuffle,"

"Well here is some ice." Kareem reached for a baggy and slid some ice cubes in it before handing it over to me.

"Thank you."

"Welcome. Tonight, just watch and learn. By the way you look familiar. Have I seen you somewhere?"

"I used to dance in Memphis maybe you saw me there once."

"No it wasn't that. I don't really like strip clubs. I'm only here helping out Czar. He's like a son to me."

"Oh well I don't know," I replied.

I prayed that he didn't recognize me from being cop. That was one of my greatest fears. That someone would recognize me from when I pulled them over years ago or something like that.

"It'll come to me," he smiled.

I hope not.

"Anyways let me show you how to run the bar. You're a pretty woman so you'll probably get more tips than I do," he laughed.

For the rest of the night I watched him mix drinks and take multiple orders. I took mental notes of how he was able to respond and serve different people at one time. This was much better than me dancing on a damn pole. By the time 2 AM rolled around, I was mixing and serving drinks on my own. It came natural for me. I had even made $500 in tips just being Kareem's side kick. If I had a few nights like this, I would be paying Eli off in no time. And I could quit hitting Nino up.

"You're a pro," Kareem complimented as the night began to wind down. We did a last call for alcohol and then started to clean up.

"You're a good teacher."

"I try. Well you can head out now. You don't have to stay until the club closes since the bar closes at 2."

"See you tomorrow night?"I asked.

"I think you may be able to fly solo Z'Cola," he joked.

I laughed him off while waiving my hand. I rushed back to the dressing room to put sundress back on before heading out of the club through the back entrance.

The cool air danced across my skin and my lungs felt lighter since I was breathing in fresh oxygen. The club smelled of cheap cologne, perfume, money and sweat. It felt good to be outside.

I hopped into the Camry and pushed the key into the ignition, however the car wouldn't start. I tried several times but nothing would work.

"Damn it," I grumbled before getting out of the car. Exhaustion had settled with in my body, leaving my eyes heavy, my body achy and my thoughts jumbled. All I wanted to do was climb into my bed. Frustrated, I stomped back into the club. On my way in, I walked past Javi and Czar who were standing towards the back talking about something in secret.

"What's wrong?" Czar asked when he noticed my scrunched-up face.

"My car won't start."

"Do you want me to get it towed?"

"Not tonight. I'm too tired to deal with that. I just want to go home and get some rest. I can get it towed tomorrow. As of right now I just want to get an Uber."

"Don't waste money on that shit. Let me give you a ride home. I'm about to leave anyway."

"Czar, you don't have to do that. Really, I'd be fine on my own."

"Girl, take the ride," Javi chimed in before breaking out into laughter.

Sucking my teeth, I rolled my eyes before refocusing my attention on Czar.

"It's nothing. Come on let's go," he said.

"Fine," I replied. I buckled easily because I knew that if I were in his car I might find a clue or a link to his illegal doings.

We piled into his brand new Lambo car.

"Where do you stay?"

"Off of Langley Road. I can direct you there," I said.

"Damn the struggle is real. Looks like you need a new car," he joked.

"Yea, but my tuition comes first," I lied.

"Of course. How much did you make in tips tonight?"

"About $500."

"That's good. Keep a total of your tips every night. By the end of the week, I'll match it and write you a check. I don't want to see someone like you working in my strip club forever."

"Well, aren't you generous. Where is this "tuition" money actually coming from?" I pried.

"If you must know, the clubs do very well. And in addition to the clubs my partner Javi and I are opening up a chain of gyms. Business is booming. Besides, I'm writing this off because it really is a scholarship donation," he laughed.

"I appreciate it." I bit the inside of my cheek because of my shame. How could I take this man's money when I'm investigating him for drug trafficking. Even though I was just doing my job,I felt foul.

"You got any kids?" he asked.

"Nope. how about you?" I returned the question. As soon as it left my lips, his jaw tensed as if it were a sensitive subject.

"No."

"Do you want them?"

"Hell yea. I'm ready to start my legacy. I need a seed to pass all of this down too."

"I see you're married," I said in response to the ring that circled around his finger.

"Yea…are you? Well clearly, you're not. What kind of man would let his woman strip."

Certainly not Kaz. If he knew that I was doing this he would have a fit. Which is why i hope this assignment is over before he wakes out of his coma.

"Nope I'm single," I further descended into my lie.

"That's crazy. You're sexy. You seem sweet so far. I even like the fact that you stood up for yourself. Bricks has been a problem for a while now."

"I had no choice. She started it and I knew that if I let it slide then the rest of those thots would make it hard for me."

"That's why I didn't fire you. I also don't want you getting caught up in no shit like that again. Steer clear of the rest of those girls. Bricks was definitely a problem but she wasn't the only one."

"I'll keep that in mind," I replied as he pulled up to my apartment.

The tension in the car was thick. My attraction to him was completely out of control. I wondered if he felt the same way. It could all be in my mind but there's something in the way his eyes glance over me. It was as if his ocean blue eyes baptized me.

"Thank you for the ride," I said as he placed the car into park.

"Of course. It's my pleasure to help hard working women out. Keep your head up. I'll have your car towed here in the morning so that you don't have to worry about it."

"That's really sweet. I appreciate that."

"You're welcome. See you tomorrow," he responded as I got out of the car. He waited until I was in the apartment before he pulled off like a true gentlemen. What were these feelings that I had for him? And how could I put them to rest. I was married woman who was in love with my husband. And to top it off, I needed to arrest him if I wanted a promotion. If I wanted to be with Nichelle, when she made commissioner, I need a big win like taking down his organization.

Chapter 17

Aria

The sunlight bounced off the aquamarine pool water in my backyard while the wind whistled between the fake palm trees. I told my husband I wanted a pool in our backyard that reminded me of Miami, and like a good puppy he obliged. If only he had stayed a good puppy. Like all dogs, he's straying, thus I'm going to have to put him down.

To ensure that Nokio does my dirty work, I have to give him treats here in there to keep him on his leash. All of these niggas were nothing but pets for me to control.

I sat in my wheelchair underneath a cabana while Nokio stood over me thrusting his dick in and out of my mouth by the poolside, living a king's dream. I can't even remember the last time Czar and I fucked, even before he found out about the abortion. He had been so busy opening up new clubs that when he finally came home at night he was too tired to fuck.

"Damn, Aria," Nokio groaned as he gripped the back of my hair, pulling at my stresses that were flowing in long loose curls.

I bobbed back and forth to meet the demands of his thrusting. Honestly, I didn't like sucking dick. I only did it when I needed to be manipulative.

"Shit. Your mouth is so wet," Nokio whispered as the tip of his dick rushed the back of my throat.

"Mhhmm, you like that?" I asked when I slid his dick from my lips and began to use my hands. I curled my fingers around his shaft and jerked passionately while looking up at him.

"Put it back in your mouth. I'm about to cum!" he announced while stabbing his dick at my face, missing the obvious hole. Niggas. It's bright outside, the sun is literally shining on us and he still can't find the hole.

Eventually, he landed back in my mouth and began to thrust even harder. Crashing his dick in and out of my mouth, liquid spilled from the sides of my mouth. Breathing became difficult and I gasped for air whenever he pulled out slightly.

"Ahhh shit, shawty!" He hollered.

Shut the fuck up. I though to myself. Our home was pretty secluded but you never know who could be driving by.

My mouth was stretched to capacity and I wasn't sure how much longer I could endure him banging against my face. However, I kept on sucking as if my life depended on it. I knew that he would be afraid to kill Czar. He could possibly back out of it and I couldn't have that.

Finally, in a matter of moments he ejaculated in my mouth. His creamy elixir spilled out of my mouth before he slowly pulled it out of me. Effortlessly, I swallowed while he backed away from my chair. I could see that he was disoriented as he wobbled to one of the pool chairs, plopping down on it like a whale out of water.

Wiping my mouth I said, "uh uh nigga, you gotta return the favor."

"Where the fuck is Czar?" he asked before reaching for a towel that sat on a table near him. He threw it over his eyes to shield them from the sun.

"He won't be coming here any time soon. So come, pick me up, lay me down and eat my pussy," I commanded.

Hesitation wafted over his body as he laid there struggling to get up. I knew that I sucked the sneaky soul out of him and that he was tired. But I didn't care. I was horny too.

"Aight shawty. I got you," he responded, finally lifting himself off of the pool chair. He marched over to me and scooped me up in his strong arms. Knees weak and buckling, he somehow managed to bring me to the chair.

Kneeling down, he lifted my yellow sundress up to see my moist pussy.

"You wore a nigga out with that head."

"I know," I quipped before running my fingers along my pussy.

"Taste it," I said while spreading my juicy lips so that he could get a clear view.

"Mhhm," he agreed before pulling my juice box close to his face. He planted his face in between my thighs and went straight for my clit. There was no need for foreplay since I couldn't feel my legs. I didn't need him sucking and licking my thighs. Only feeling there was below my legs, was my pussy. If I had lost sensation there, I probably would have killed myself.

"Yes, suck on my clit," I moaned as he tugged at my hot button with his warm lips. My heart be sped up while my eyes rolled up towards the open sky before retreating to the back of my head.

Biting down on my bottom lip, I pushed his face closer into my pussy.

"Finger fuck me!" I commanded, forcing him to glide his index and middle fingers into my beckoning cave. As soon as he entered me I lost all control. Massaging my g-spot, I had the overwhelming urge to bust all over his hand.

My spine arched while I listened to his slurping sounds and I forced my nails into his skin.

"Hmmmm," he grunted at the pleasurable pain. "Cum for me," he continued.

Doing just that, I squirted even more powerful than the fountain in my garden. My flood drowned his face as he continued going causing me chest to quiver.

"Damn Aria," he said as he pulled his finger out of me. He lifted his hand so that we could both see my glistening essence underneath the sun.

"Thank you," I breathed.

"I don't even feel like talking about business now." He was exasperated.

"You don't have a choice. Do you want this empire or not?"

"Of course," he replied while wiping his face with the towel. I then watched him as he wheeled my chair close to me. Pretending to be like a gentleman he tugged my dress down so that I was covered and then lifted me up, placing me down in the chair.

Plopping down on the pool chair beside me, he cupped his face and let out a billowing yawn.

"I'll make you some coffee in a bit. First let's discuss the plan," I began.

"I'm all ears."

"When I went through Czar's files, I was able to get his passwords to his cell phones. I contacted them and got a copy of all recent text messages. There will be a drop in a week. We need to get a crew and plan a shoot out. It needs to look like it's one of Czar's and of course Czar has to be the one to get shot. If his connect sees that his people are in discourse, they will be looking for a new distributor. We'll then assemble an old team. I can get some of my father's old workers, and will take over Czar's territory. Can you get a crew?"

"Yea, I guess I can. What do I tell them when they ask why are we killing Czar?"

"Good question, sweetie," I smirked while digging into my purse.

"You can show him this. This is proof that he's getting out of the game thus won't be needing their services anymore. They are already underpaid, just like you. With Czar out the game, how will they eat?" I replied to his question by showing him the message between Czar and Javi. The text message stated that they would buying up more gyms and clubs so that they could make money legitimately.

How dare Czar. Did he even think about me in all of this. I deserved to be the wife of a boss, not the owner of titty clubs and sweaty gyms. Fuck him! He's going to learn to day.

"Aight, sounds like a plan. I'll get to work on that crew now," he answered.

My peach stained lips parted into a sinister grin as I thought about my plan falling into action. No one would expect this from a bitch who couldn't even walk. Never discount a woman's weaknesses. We'll always use them as strengths.

Chapter 18

Apryl

Weeks were rolling by and I still hadn't discovered any evidence of drugs trafficking. Czar was really good at cleaning up his tracks and disposing of any proof that he was even dealing. Good for him. Bad for me. Pressure from Nichelle was weighing on me heavily.

"You've got to find me something soon or I have to pull you out. If I pull you out there is no way they're going to let you join me if I make police commissioner let alone be detective," she said in our last conversation.

I needed to find something soon however, I was conflicted. Czar had grown on me like a wild vine. There was definitely chemistry between us. I knew that he was feeling me every single time he handed me over cash that matched my tips. This was too messy of a situation. If he found out who I really was he would hate me.

"Wassup, Cola," Javi greeted me when I walked into the club. It was the middle of the afternoon on a Monday, the day the club was typically closed. Czar and Javi called for a staff meeting to discuss upcoming events.

"Hey Javi," I greeted as I made my way into the club. Sunshine lit up the outside of the club, but once I crossed the threshold I stepped into dimness. I hated being in there doing the day because of that contrast. One of my personal beliefs is, if it's warm and the sun is shining then you should be outside to enjoy it, not in some dark dank night club.

"Aight, afternoon everyone," Czar greeted. "Today I wanted to discuss some upcoming events that the club is putting on so that we can expand the brand. Next month rapper Dab and Yolo Savage are coming here to do a private party. I need for this place to be top notch for them since they will be bringing in a lot high-end clientele. Also we'll be throwing our annual pool party."

"We don't have a pool," Nino the bouncer chimed in. Everyone chuckled under their breath but Czar didn't look amused.

"The party will be at a new social club that I'm opening called Deluxe Lounge. There will be a huge pool there. I need some help planning the party. Cola, I was thinking that you can partner with me on that? How does that sound?"

"Wow that works for me."

"I figured you'd need some kind of management experience since you'll be majoring in business management in college."

"I appreciate you looking out for me," I replied but my heart sank. This man was doing so much for me but I was a big liar.

While I continued to over think my lies, he dispersed other tasks that needed to be done.

Once the meeting ended everyone got up ready to leave so that we could enjoy the rest of our day off. I had to have a secret meeting with Andre to give him an update.

"Can I speak to you for a moment, Cola?"

"Yea whats up?" I asked. He motioned his head towards his office, I followed behind.

"There's a party planner by the name of Maya Monroe. I want to book her for the pool party. I think you're smart and well-spoken enough to link up with her. I trust that you're responsible enough to get the ball rolling and work with her to have a great event.

"Of course," I responded while he began to scroll through his phone. When his hand clutched at his phone I noticed that he wasn't wearing his wedding ring.

Not thinking I boldly asked, "Where is your ring?"

Startled by nerve, he look down at his ring before shaking his head.

"My wife and I are going through something."

"What if you don't mind me asking?"

"It's complicated. I want children. She doesn't. She had a secret abortion and I recently found out about it."

Biting down on my bottom lip, I sighed. Kaz and I wanted children badly too but because of my endometriosis, we found out it might not happen. Admittedly we began to grow apart when we found out I would be fertility challenged. It was one of the reasons he decided to go to law school since he figured he would have more time and energy on his hands without babies.

Since I felt guilty, I decided to support him in his endeavors by footing the bill which put me in a bind. I had to give up my wedding band and engagement ring to Eli who I still owed $10,000 too. Luckily, I had most of the money from the tips and cash that Czar gave me. Not to mention I was still getting cash from Nino.

"Did you ask her why she did such a thing?"

"I did but honestly there is no answer that would make it ok. I give her everything. And the shit got me out here looking dumb. I bought her a fuckin' house I don't even like. She has a whole room dedicated to just shoes. So in my opinion she should feel comfortable enough to tell me she didn't want kids. Don't just take the option away from me."

"Do you still love her?"

"Of course, I do. I just don't know if I could be with a liar. Little lies I can forgive but killing my seed. There's no forgiving that," he confessed, making me feel even worse.

"I think you should talk to her. Find out why she lied. It could be something major that you can work through." I swept a tendril of the auburn wig out of my face.

"You're so different from the rest of these broads."

"How do you mean?"

"You ain't thirsty. You're trying to better yourself. You're professional. You're taking yourself and not trying to land a baller. I like it. It's refreshing. Most of the women in my life, my wife included won't deal with a nigga who is on the come up. They want him to have it made already."

If only he knew.

"There's plenty of us out there. And as for your wife, you knew how she was when you met her. You have to accept for who she is or divorce her. But first, try to understand why she killed your baby."

"You're right."

"I'm starving do you want to get something to eat? Maybe it will get ease your mind."

"Yea, that works," he said before standing up.

I swear whenever that man moved around me, something stirred within. He had undeniable swag and sex appeal. Why in the hell would his wife abort their child? As bad as I wanted a baby, I could never do such a thing to my husband. Speaking of my husband, I needed to check in on him. Since I was undercover I couldn't really visit him. I had to lay low and not see my friends and family until the assignment was complete.

Chapter 19

Mayeka

The warmth of the sun bled through the blinds to comfort my baby boy who was laying in his crib. Before walking out of his room I planted a gentle kiss on his cheek while he napped. I then left his room to finish the loads of laundry that taunted me, waiting for me to return to the living room just so I could spend the rest of the day folding clothes.

I was beyond tired and hadn't got much sleep since the night I thought I was going to lose my son. That night when Eli came over he had a seizure. After a series of tests it was determined that he was epileptic. I was able to administer mouth to mouth resuscitation on him, and got him breathing on his own. But the fact that that monster Eli, ran out of my house after not even letting me check on my son, didn't sit well with me.

"What the fuck Mayeka! I had to leave my wife in the middle of the night! She showed up to my office the next day. This shit is a fucking mess! You have to do better!" Braxton fussed at me while I folded clothes.

I placed BJ's onesies, t-shirts, overalls and pants in the drawer while I ignored his yelling. The scent of baby powder that drifted through the air kept me calm. Braxton's voice traveled through one ear and out the other.

"Do you even hear me talking to you?!"

"What the fuck do you want me to do? He has epilepsy. I didn't know he was going to have a seizure in the middle of the night. And of course I had to call you because BJ is on your damn health insurance! I'm sorry that the son you laid down with me to make is such an inconvenience to that damn wife of yours. If you would leave the bitch and be here with me, this could've been prevented!" I hollered back.

Angrily, I threw a pair of socks at his face as if that were going to harm him. Since they were fresh out of the dryer they had static and stuck to his face.

Braxton sighed, before pulling the socks off his face and placing them back down on the couch.

"You know I can't do that baby. Not right now. I'm a shoe in for the primaries. Once that's over, then I know I can win the campaign. And when I'm the mayor of this city, I promise I will be with you. You just have to let me work this out," he replied.

I shook my head in disbelief while tossing down the rest of the clothes that I was trying to neatly fold. I didn't believe him. I knew the only way that he was going to leave his wife is if the bitch and those daughters all died.

"You don't believe me."

"I find it hard to believe. I just need you here. Sometimes, I don't feel safe being here alone." That was the truth. I knew that Eli would be back.

"What do you mean you don't feel safe? Is someone following you or threatening you."

My tongue became too numb to respond. I couldn't tell him about Eli because then I would have to tell him why Eli was following me. He couldn't know that I may have killed someone with his car.

"No. It's just that this city can get crazy. And it's hard living alone as a woman with a baby. That's all."

"You're safe. But if it will make you feel any safer than, I will get a new security system installed in here. I'll get you security cameras and we might be able to get you a gun."

"Now you know I got that felony charge. No one is going to give me a gun," I replied.

"I'll buy it in my name. How does that sound?" He asked me while stroking my cheek.

"Fine."

"Aight. I gotta head home. Are you going to be ok?

"Ugh. Just leave," I spat before pushing him away. I was sick and tired of him coming in and out of my house. This nigga was all talk and I needed way more action. If he couldn't spend more time with me and BJ, then I was going to have to make some changes.

"I told you I'm sorry," he spat.

"I hear you. I need to do this house work. We'll talk later," I replied, before leading him towards the front door.

He leaned in for a kiss but being the petty bitch that I am, I lifted my hand, squeezed his lips then mushed him in the face.

"Whatever," he grunted before pulling at the front door and walking out.

Turning around I marched back to the clothes that I was folding and in a rage I tore them from the couch and threw them to the ground. Like a maniac I walked around my beautiful condo, and began ripping pictures and paintings from the walls and hurling them to the floor, shattering the glass all around. Angry and tired of being alone, I had to find away to claim Braxton. He couldn't know it was my doing though. Because let's say, I got rid of his wife, he would never forgive me. I needed to think of something, and think of it quick.

* * *

Hours later, the sun had exited stage left and allowed the moon to get its shine. After my bratty moment, I had calmed down my drinking a few glasses of wine. BJ had woke up and was hungry, so I had fed him and let him play on his floor while I watched. I was too tired to clean up the mess that I had made in the living room, so I had to let him loose on the floor of his room.

I sat in the rocking chair in his nursery, nursing glasses of moscato while watching over him.

"You look just like him." The words staggered out of mouth. The wine had loosened my tongue and relaxed my face. It probably wasn't the best idea to be drinking while watching my child, but fuck it I needed a drink.

"Whaaaaa," BJ began to cry, interrupting my drunken stupor. I sat the wine glass down and lifted him up before bringing him to his changing table. I knew it was about that time for him to get a new diaper.

After changing his diaper, I brought him in the kitchen with me so that I could fix me something to eat. The liquor was starting to sour in my stomach making realize that I hadn't eaten anything since before Braxton left my house. Placing my son in his swing, I scoured through my refrigerator for food to make. Locating a NY strip steak, I decided to make me steak and potatoes. I pulled out an onion and green pepper to trim the meat with, and reached for my butcher knife and began to chop.

My mind was all over the place, thinking of ways to get rid of his wife so that he could be with me and BJ full time. And since I was completely unfocused, I not only chopped onions and green peppers but my own fucking finger.

"OW!" I shouted when the blade ripped into my flesh.

The sound of giggling filled the kitchen. "Oh you think that's funny little boy," I teased when I turned around to see his toothless smile. He was only four months and I knew he didn't know what was happening. He heard mommy make a strange sound and it made him smile.

I suckled on my finger to stop the bleeding while looking for a band aid. When I finally found one, I couldn't' do anything but smile at my son. Seeing his lips widen to reveal his gummy grim always warmed my heart. I would do anything for that little boy.

Just as I wrapped the band aid around my finger, someone knocked on my door. Knowing I wasn't expecting anyone, I ignored it but the knocking continued.

"Who the fuck is it?" I grumbled when I stomped to the front door.

"It's the big bad wolf! Let me in, let me in!" Eli's voice snarled from the other side.

I inhaled an exhaled deeply.

"I can't do that tonight. Come back tomorrow," I said, not wanting to be bothered right then or any other time by this nigga.

"You know that's not how this works. If I can't come in when I want to then I'll go to the police when I want to."

"Shit!" I hissed before turning the lock and allowing him in.

"Can you at least call before you come?"

"I made sure your little boyfriend wasn't here," he spat before walking in.

"Let me put my son down," I said as I closed the door behind him.

"Yea, how is he? I'm sorry about the other night. I just didn't want to be here when the ambulance got here."

"Fuck you for that by the way! My son could have died!"

"Well he didn't."

How could someone be so callous? This man was a monster. I thought to myself as I knelt down to my son, handing him a pacifier.

"What the hell happened in here?" Eli asked from the living room referring to the mess I had made.

"Nothing." That nigga didn't need to know my business. As he walked out of the living room he wandered his disgusting ass into my kitchen.

"Oh you were about to cook me a steak?" He asked me when he saw the NY strip sitting on the counter.

"Nigga, please," I scoffed.

"Oh I think you should be nicer to me considering, I hold your life in my hands," he spoke as he slithered near.

My skin crawled as if a thousand spiders danced underneath. The sizzle of the steak filled the air, mixing with his breath. I really hated that this is what my life had become. Apart of me would rather sit in jail for hitting that man than to have to fuck Eli again.

"I'm sorry," I whispered.

"That's more like it."

He walked closer, and extended his hands, wrapping them around my waist. My stomach coiled and my mouth became extremely dry.

"Come on, I don't have all night. I have to get back to work," he said pulling me closer.

Begrudgingly obeying him, I decided to turn down the fire on the steak.

"Let's go to the room," I suggested, not wanting to bother my son who had fallen asleep with the pacifier in his mouth.

"No, I want you right here," he grunted.

"Please let's go into my bedroom, my son is right there," I pleaded.

"I don't give a fuck. He aint my son," he barked before yanking me close. He ripped off my clothes and tossed me to the ground like a rag doll. Embarrassment reddened my face and tears dripped from my eyes.

"Eli please leave me alone!"

"I told you I don't have to fuck around," he spat as he came down to the ground. He pulled me on to my hands knees. My body shook in terror while I fought to get away. Strongarming me, he grabbed me by my neck.

"Usually I like it when you're feisty, but today I'm in a rush. I can't be playing hard to get with you," he spoke in my ear as he unzipped his jeans. The sound of him undoing his pants made me cringe. Tears streamed down my face as he forced his dick inside of me.

"Ahhhh, please!" I hollered to the top of my lungs but he wouldn't get off of me.

The commotion caused BJ to stir in his sleep and eventually he woke up. He wailed in unison with me. How could this nigga do this in front of my baby. I hated him so much and I wanted him to die.

Eventually, I blanked out. My mind went some place else to escape Eli raping me and my baby screaming. Hot tears seared my cheeks while the aroma of the seared steak stirred in the room. I swear on everything that I love that I will kill this nigga when I get a chance. Roughly, he banged into me. The hard kitchen tiled floor was painful against my knees and shins.

Eventually he came, bustin' his nut all over my back per the usual.

"Got damn Honey Bunz!" He growled and grunted. Drops of sweat fell from him onto my back, mixing in with this nut. My knees scraped against the kitchen floor as he stood up from me, stretching as if he had just put in work. BJ's shrills filled the air, sounding like an ambulance siren, loud and alarming.

I laid on the floor curled into a tight ball while I wept. I was too distraught to even tend to my son.

"Whew," Eli sighed as he walked over to my steak.

This nigga had the audacity to put my steak on a plate and sit down at my table.

"Let met get into this before I head out," he said as I heard him cut into the steak. He sat there eating my food while I laid there trembling. Sore, I struggled to stand up from the floor. I picked up my son and disappeared into the bathroom where I tried to clean myself up and comfort him.

Together BJ and I cried while Eli finished eating my dinner. After he was done, he left without saying a word. I had to make sure this never happened again .

Chapter 20

Apryl

Nicki Minaj's "No Frauds" blasted through the Sweet Suite's speakers while patrons clamored to get to the front of the club. Tonight the club was hosting some of the top dancers in the country for it's annual competition. From one end of the club to the other, it was packed with visitors, locals, thugs, corporate dudes, and even lots of women.

I stood to make a shit load of cash in tips tonight. Depending on how much I made, I might even be able to stop extorting Nino. I just wanted to be a straight laced cop.

"Can I get a Henny and a Coke?" A voice said from behind me after I finished, placing a few bottles of Ace of Spades in the fridge.

"Sure, coming right..." I was startled when I turned around to see who it was asking me for the drink. It was Nino.

"What the fuck are you doing here bartending? Is this some kinda set up?" he barked. Luckily, no one could hear him. There was another bartender working with me tonight but she was on the other end the bar.

"Shhh! Shut up! And no I'm not setting anyone up!" I lied as I stomped from around the counter.

"Fuck that! I was paying you to keep me out the streets. Now you working here? Bitch you're a foul cop! You working this place undercover and you extorting me. Fuckin' dirty pig!"

"Stop! Please let's go outside. Let's talk about it? You can't blow up my spot."

"Fine come on then," he seethed, grabbing my arm and forcing me outside through the back door. We walked outside of the club where the smell of stale cigarette smoked smacked me in my face. Cigarette and Swisher butts littered the ground since this is where a lot of the girls went to smoke for their breaks. The cool night air was still and didn't do anything to push the smell away.

"Explain your moutherfuckin' self right now before I go tell Czar and he put fuckin' bullet in your head."

"Listen. I didn't know you were affiliated with Czar. I didn't know that Czar was in the drug game. I swear!" I lied through my damn teeth. Well, I didn't know that Nino worked for Czar.

"Bitch, you lyin'"

"No, I'm not. I'm working here because I need the cash. That's why I was hitting you up for money. Please look, my husband is dying!" I cried while flashing a picture of Kazman laying in the hospital bed with tubes running in and out of his nose.

Nino snatched the phone from me and examined it closely.

"That's your husband? Where your wedding ring?"

"I had to pawn it. It cost so much money to keep him in the hospital. I have to work here and hit you for cash. Please don't tell Czar, I don't want to die. If I die no one will be able to take care of my husband and they'll pull the plug. The doctors are saying there is a chance that he could wake up. Please," I began to cry.

"Look, bitch, if Czar find out you a cop and that I knew you were a cop, I'm just as good as dead. So here is what you're gonna do. You're going to help me get out of Atlanta."

"Help you how?"

"Listen, I'm on probation. I can't leave the state unless my probationary officer, testifies to a judge. I need you to talk to him. My daughter is in Florida and that's where I want to be."

My tongue laid in my mouth arid as the ashes that were sprinkled on the concrete outside. Attempting to compose myself, I took several deep breaths in and out before clearing my throat to speak.

"There is no way I can guarantee that but I will talk to him. Ok? Who is your P.O.?"

"Mercy Louis."

"Fuck!" I grunted when I heard the name. Mercy and I went had a length history together and I knew she wouldn't listen to me. But I had to see what I can do.

"I'll do my best. When is your next hearing?"

"In a month."

"Ok," I replied before walking away.

"Yo, if you don't deliver. I'm snitchin'. And I don't care who gets your first, the feds or Czar. Actually, you better hope it's the Feds. They won't go as hard as Czar will."

"I got you. Let me work." His words pierced my core like a knife. I didn't know how I was going to convince Mercy Louis to let Nino go to Florida. That bitch hated me.

Just as I walked away, I pulled out my phone to see if I had any messages. Lo and behold I did. There were several missed calls from Andre and finally a text message that read: "I need to talk to you a.s.a.p."

Nino brushed past me while I read the message. Placing the phone to my ear, I was about to call Dre to see what was going on but then Czar walked outside.

Damn it.

"I gotta say thank you for

"You takin' a phone break right now, while half the city is in there tonight?" Czar asked playfully. His blue eyes looked like infinity pools underneath the moonlight.

"No, it was just a little emergency."

"Yea it happens. Is everything ok?"

"No I actually have to leave. It's my sister, she's sick."

"Oh shit. Go handle your business, shawty. I'll see you later, ok? And don't worry about the tips. I will make you have some money tonight. I know how important paying that tuition is," he winked.

"Thank you so much," I replied.

* * *

An hour later, I had met up with Andre at our police headquarters. Since it was after hours, the office was void of any people, the lights were off except for the emergency lights and the computer monitors.

"What's going on? You called me off duty and you know how risky that is?" I spat, knowing damn well that I was in a crazy ass bind with Nino.

"I have something to show you. Something that's going to blow your fucking mind. I found out who hit Kazman," he said as he got up and grabbed a disc. He slipped the DVD into his computer player.

"I had my buddy in surveillance dig up the tape because apparently, someone had it deleted."

"What tape?"

"The place where he was hit had a camera on the light pole. Someone had it deleted. And I think I have an idea who," Dre said before hitting play.

"What are you talking about?"

"Just watch," he said.

The grainy video had a sepia filter, thus it was hard to see. I focused my eyes on the video to make sure I could see who had hit my husband and had him laying in a coma fighting for his life. Suddenly, Kaz appeared but he wasn't alone. Instead, he was with a woman and they were holding hands.

"What the fuck?"

"Keep watching," Andre instructed.

Doing as Andre asked me, I watched Kaz turn to the woman and plant his lips on her. They kissed for a few seconds.

"You see who that is?" Andre asked as I squinted my eyes to see. It became clear as day that the bitch he was kissing was no other but my *friend* and boss, Nichelle.

"Oh my god!" I cupped my mouth in disbelief. Nichelle stepped away from Kaz to tie her shoe and then Kaz stumbles a bit into the street.

And like a bat out of hell a Mercedes comes and smashes right into him, slows down a bit and then keeps going.

"That's a silver 2017 Mercedes," Andre said...

"My brother-in-law has a car like that."

"Exactly. It was your brother-in-law," Andre responded when he whipped out a zoomed in picture of the license plate.

"What the fuck?" My bottom lip quivered as I tried to take it all in. My husband was cheating on me with Nichelle and my brother in law hit him? Nothing was adding up.

"Yep. It looks like Braxton Nicks hit your husband. Maybe he knew that Kaz was cheating. I don't know. What's clear is this; after he was hit Nichelle ran off. Presumably she is the one who called 911 but I haven't been able to locate the tape.

Tear by tear trickled down my face at the realization that my husband was cheating on me. After all of the sacrifices I have made for this man, how could he do this to me. I was taking care of him; paying all of our bills, cooking the food, cleaning the house. All so that he could study, yet he was fucking my boss! I was risking my career by extorting that nigga Nino, just so that he could switch careers.

Rage blazed in my chest making me so hot that sweat beaded across my brow. My vision became blurry and my tongue was stiff and dry, feeling like asphalt in my mouth.

"Apryl?" Andre called out my name before sliding his arm around my shoulders.

"I want to kill him! I hate him so much right now. I want him dead," I shouted. My fist balled tightly and I slammed them in the desk before walking away.

"Hold up." Andre ran after me.

"What?!"

"Don't do anything stupid. You didn't do anything wrong. You're good in all of this so don't fuck it up," Andre attempted to comfort me, completely unaware of my arrangement with Nino.

"I'm going to HR! This has to be a violation!" I cried.

"You could do that but the would mess up your chances at getting a promotion on the future. Let me take care of this for you."

"How?"

"Don't worry about it. I'll think of something. Ok? You have to calm down. Take a few days off from working undercover and lay low. Just take a breather before you get back in there. Can you do that for me?" Andre asked while stroking my cheek.

"I can try."

"I'm serious. Don't confront Nichelle nor Braxton. I know that you and your sister are close but Cipriana can't know either. Got it?"

"Got it," I mumbled while tears escaped down my face. Andre left the office and returned with some tissues for me to dry my eyes.

"Thank you," I spat.

"You're welcome. It's going to be ok. I'll make it right."

I wasn't sure how he was going to fix this issue but one thing I knew for sure was, if and when Kazman woke up, I was punching him in the damn face and asking for a divorce. There was no way in hell I would stay with a man who used me like this.

Chapter 21

Cipriana

"I told you, you needed to lose weight if you expected to keep a man like that." My mother's calloused words made my heart stop beating.

She made it seem as if I had brought this on myself. Somehow my expanding waistline, pushed my husband out of our house in the middle of the night to fuck someone else. If she weren't my mother I would have slapped the taste out of her mouth.

Instead I responded with, "Thank you for watching the kids. I have to go," I replied before walking towards my daughters to give them a kiss and hug goodbye.

Tonight I was going to seriously confront my husband. I refused to stay in this marriage another minute. His emotional abuse was weighing me down and pretty soon it would affect the kids. His actions were already causing them to be taken out of private school.

"Good luck, CiCi!" My mother called out to me as I walked out of the house.

Fuck her. And as for that weight loss shit, ever since I've been working with Javi, I had seen a vast improvement. Too bad she was too selfish and rude to see that I had lose 20lbs already.

I hopped in my car and drove to STK meet Javi. Today we were doing lunch together since it was one of my rest days. There was something about him that I was falling for although I knew I shouldn't. He probably only wanted to fuck me anyway. What would he want with an overweight woman with three children, anyway?

As I rode towards our lunch spot, I received phone call from an unrecognizable number. Knowing that it could be anyone or anything pertaining to my kids, I answered the phone.

"Hello this is Cipriana Nicks speaking."

"Hi Cipriana this Knowledge Santiago, of SanRo pProductions. I wanted to discuss your book *"If These Walls Could Talk"*, you sent it to us about a month ago and we read it and would like to discuss buying the rights from you. We'd like to turn it into a film.

"Oh my god!" My heart skipped a beat.

"Do you have time next week to meet to discuss this in detail?" His baritone voice hummed into my ear.

"I do."

"Good shit. I'll email you the details. I look forward to meeting with you and hopefully bringing your vision to the big screen."

Floating on cloud nine I drove away to link up with Javi. Knowledge Santiago was a film producer who was on the come up. He had moved to New York then to DC before finally settling in Atlanta with his long-term girlfriend Maya. He had already produced a few different television shows and now he was branching off into movies. When I found out about him, I sent my book so that he could see if he would turn it into a movie.

This good news sent me flying high. I couldn't wait to tell Javi. It was a shame I couldn't even share it with my own husband. It's not like he ever believed in my dreams anyway.

When I arrived at STK I parked the car and walked out confidently. I was wearing a navy blue sundress with striped white and blue wedges, and red jewelry as my accent pieces. I had beat my face and was wearing Ruby Woo red lipstick from Mac. It felt good to finally take care of myself and get spruced up.

The truth is, I did it for Javi. I loved the way he looked at me. It was as if he gave me an incentive to get dolled up. Ever since I met him, each day I became more and more confident.

"Damn shawty," I heard Javi's voice say as soon as I entered the restaurant.

My eyes adjusted to the dimness of the restaurant while I tried to spot him out. When I turned around, I saw him sitting on the bench waiting for me.

"I'm sorry I'm running late," I said when I spotted him.

"It's all good. I just got here myself. But shit, I don't' even want nothing to eat if it don't involve you on the menu," he complimented. He stood up from the bench and reached towards me to give me a hug. It felt relaxing to be in his embrace. Aside from hugs from my daughters, I didn't receive much affection that I desperately craved.

"You better stop…"

"Why? You about to leave your husband for me," he flirted.

"Boy please," I bashfully smiled. As much as I would have loved to leave Braxton, I knew that for the sake of my girls and his mayoral campaign that wasn't feasible.

"You should…"

"Is this your date?" the hostess interrupted us.

"Yep," Javi responded.

"Ok right this way."

Javi and I both followed the petite woman to our booth. I playfully nudge him before whispering, "This is not a date. We are just friends."

"Yea right."

We sat down at the booth. As I searched the menu, I felt his eyes lock into my body, making me uncomfortable.

"What?" I asked, raising my eyebrow.

"You're too amazing to be with the nigga. You never told me what happened when you went to his office that day."

"I don't want to get into that. I have some really good news though,"

"Aight I won't pry. Just know that nigga ain't shit and you can do better. But what's your good news?"

"Knowledge Santiago called me from SanRo Productions and he wants to meet with me to discuss turning my book into a movie!"

"Oh shit! I'm so proud of you shawty! That's hot. Baby girl gon be the next Ava Duvernay! When did you find out?"

"Right before I came over here! I'm so ecstatic," I replied smiling ear to ear.

"I bet. You deserve it. I loved your book by the way. Well, let's celebrate! Imma get you a bottle of champagne," he announced.

"No Javi. I can't drink in the middle of the day."

"Yes you can. I'll help you sober up after," he replied before waiving a server over. He ordered a bottle of champagne, lobster and steak for us both and scallops for an appetizer.

An hour later we were full on decadent food, buzzed from expensive bubbly and worn out. My eyes searched over the table, looking at the left-over deliciousness. While I tried to deny that this was a date, it was a date and it was the best date I had been on in a long time. I don't think Braxton has taken me out since before Zoe was born. I can't believe that Javi care enough to do this.

"You didn't have to do all of this." I shyly shook my head. As soon as the words left my mouth he reached for my hand and held it tightly.

"Someone needs to do all of this for you. Your babies are too young to appreciate you yet. Your husband is too much of a fuck boy."

His words warmed my heart so much that a few tears of joy and pain rushed down my face. He was right. I was completely under appreciated.

Javi got up from his side of the table and came to sit next to me. He reached in and lovingly placed his lips where my tear drops fail. It was the sweetest kiss I had ever received. He was literally kissing my pain away.

"Let's get out of here."

"We had three bottles of champagne, I can't drive," I replied.

"I can. You can sleep it off at my house," he suggested.

Not using my best judgement, I nodded yes. Without a doubt, I knew that I would get to his house and want to make love to him. I needed him to fuck me. And before this moment, I was still not completely confident that he felt the same way about me.

"Ok," I replied.

Leaving my car in the parking lot of STK we headed out and made our way to his home.

* * *

"Wow," I exclaimed as I took in the grandiose sight of his home. Who knew that owning a gym could be this lucrative. Perhaps, I was in the wrong business. Javi had the type of palace that looked like it belonged in a movie, yet here it was tucked away in the Atlanta neighhborhood of Druid Hills.

"And how many gyms do you own?" I playfully asked him as he guided me past the roman columns that framed the double stained glass doors.

"Ha! Just the one for right now. I also co-own a chain of clubs," he replied.

I followed behind him, staggering side to side due to the liquor swishing through my veins. Being a mother of three didn't allow me the opportunity to get wasted in the middle of the day, popping champagne bottles. Despite that, I was happy to indulge.

"How are you feeling? Do you want some water?" He asked me after turning on the lights in his kitchen.

"Sure. Do you live here alone?"

"Yep."

"Why so much space for one man?" I asked while ogling his chocolate skin as it glinted under the kitchen lights. His kitchen was pristine like something from a home showcase, as if it had never been used.

"Why not?" he winked, handing me over a bottle of water.

I sipped slowly on the cool water, remembering that at some point I had to leave to pick up the girls.

"You play pool?" he asked.

"No, never learned."

"Follow me."

He walked me downstairs to his recreation room that was comprised of a mini theater, pool table and a bar.

"Nice bachelor pad, you have here."

"Thank you," he replied while placing the cue balls inside the triangle. He grabbed a couple of pool sticks and handed me one before placing the other one down.

"Let me give you a quick tutorial," he announced as he stood behind me.

"Uh huh." My body heat began to rise and my nerves rattled as his closeness. He pressed into me and gripped my fingers around the pool stick.

"You nervous?" He asked.

"No."

"Relax your grip shawty. You gotta get lose," he whispered, while pulling my fingers off the stick.

"Hmmm," a moan slipped out of my lips without my approval.

"I got you moaning and you only holding my stick," he chuckled. "You ain't seen nothing yet," he continued.

He suckled on my ear, licking the inside and trailing his wet tongue down my neck. The masculine and undeniably intoxicating scent of his cologne filled my nostrils.

"I want to fuck you so bad right now," he confessed.

"Right here?" I asked as warmth pooled between my legs, soaking my already wet panties.

"Hell yes. Right here, right now."

He walked me closer to the pool table and began to hungrily kiss and suck on my juicy bottom lip. He bit down gently.

I moaned as my pussy begin to cream. His strong hands lifted me and placed me onto the pool table. I was relieved that I wasn't too heavy for him. Standing in front of me, he spread my legs and positioned himself between them.

My sumptuous thighs emitted heat and passion, tempting him to plunge into me right away.

My curious fingers reached underneath his shirt and I pressed my fingers into his firm flesh while his tongue swiveled down my neck and his hands cupped my breasts. His dick hardened with anticipation and pressed at the seam of his Balmain jeans, as if it were forcing its way out to meet my sweet juice box.

He lifted my dress and revealed my red lacy panties. He pulled away from me to take in the view of my succulent pussy that waited.

"Why are you nervous?" He asked sensing that I was panicking.

"Because the lights are on. I don't like fucking with the lights on."

"Why not," he asked, his eyes lowering on my thick thighs.

I raised my hands too ashamed to state the reason why. I didn't want to admit out loud that I didn't like my stretch marks and cellulite.

"Listen, I love your body. And whatever the fuck you are insecure about you need to let the shit go and let me work. I want you with the damn lights on. And fuck how you feel about it." He grinned

"Mhmmm," I moaned.

He licked his lips and moved forward between my legs once more. With his two rough fingers, he gently touched my clit that was pulsating in anticipation for him to touch, lick and envelop.

Finally, he pulled my dress over my head, unveiling my lavish body.

"Mhmmm, your body is bad, baby," he groaned as he threw the sundress to the ground and gently laid me down onto the pool table. I rested against the green felt cloth while I stared at the chandelier above us.

He knelt down and pulled the soaked panties from my body, tossing them to the side. Placing his face in between my thick thighs, he suckled and kissed my flesh. He merged his salivating tongue to my womanly folds as I breathed heavily. All the angst of the day vanished within a matter of moments.

He fixed his succulent lips around my clit, causing me to moan and arch my spine, my lower back pressing against that pool table. I sank my fingers into his hair, pressing into his scalp as he pressed his hands into my fleshy thighs.

"Your pussy tastes so good," he moaned as he continued to lap me up with his

tongue.

He darted his wet pulsating tongue into me, savoring the delectable taste of my honeypot. His eager tongue alternated between my clit to his lips.

"Yes baby! God yes." My body quaked as my ecstasy came to a boiling point. I shook and vibrated all over his pool table.

He came up for air, his face coated with my essence. He gawked at my naked body that was sprawled amongst the table as he gently guided me to the edge.

He unzipped his pants, finally freeing his 11-inch dick. My eyes grew large to take in the sight. It was exactly what I needed.

"Are you ready to take this dick?" he asked, holding his thick monster at my precipice.

"Yes, baby, fuck me right now," I moaned.

Every iota of tension had escaped my body. Nothing mattered in that hot and heavy moment. Not my husband, not his mysterious mistress, not my children and not even my mean mother.

The only thing that mattered was being in Xavier's masterful clutch. Repositioning himself, he pressed his dick at my pussy. Spreading my thick thighs even further, he entered into me, my pussy gripping at the entirety of his girth. I clawed at his forearm as he began to fill my pussy.

My wet walls widened to accommodate his rod as he began to further fuck my pain away. Any residual sadness or anxiety was zapped into oblivion. His body pressed onto mine was the greatest medicine.

"Yes, baby! Fuck me harder," I cried out as he leaned down and melded his firm torso into my plush body. I threw my arms around him, holding him in close, as he bit down on my scapula.

Pressing his fingers into my flesh, he growled, "Take this dick, Ci."

Unable to speak, I moaned as my eyes rolled to the back of my head.

His hard body slammed into my comforting thighs while he choked me at the same time.

"Let me hit that shit from behind," he grunted.

"Mhhhmm, yes," I cried.

He lifted away from my body, his cock coated in my creaminess.

Helping me from the table, he turned me around. I gripped at the soft leather rail around the pool table in preparation for him to continue banging my back out.

He gripped at my bodacious ass and began to tease my pussy from behind by rubbing the tip my swollen, glistening clit.

"Is this pussy mine?" he asked.

"Yes, baby, this pussy is all yours," I whimpered.

"Bend over," he demanded.

Doing as he told, I leaned forward and arched my spine for him to gain access to my succulent cunt. He caressed my voluminous breasts, unable to contain them with his hands. He gently pushed me over onto the green felted pool table as I arched my spine.

He plunged his veiny, bulging dick into my cunt and began to pump back and forth as he fucked me on the table. Once again, he wrapped his fingers around my neck while my breasts rubbed up against the table. I extended my arms and clawed at the cloth as he rammed into me.

"Come right now for me," he commanded as he pumped harder, swiveling his hips, ensuring that he hit every aspect of my walls and my g-spot.

Each time he penetrated my g-spot, I shrilled in satisfaction. Within a matter of moments, I came all over his dick. Convulsing and shaking all over the table, my pussy gripped his rod. I clamped down on his shaft while he bit his lip as he watched me vibrantly orgasm. In a matter of moments he squirted inside of me. My pussy squeezed his rod, drinking in his essence.

Sweat streamed down his face as he rose away from my body. Breathing erratically, he nakedly went to grab a towel to clean up.

Legs wobbly, I attempted to stand upright. He walked back over to me and I pulled him into my body, giving him a hug.

"You know I have to leave?" I breathless said.

"I know. Let's at least take a shower before I take you back to your car," he whispered before kissing me.

I guess if my husband can cheat, I can too.

Chapter 22

Mayeka

"Girl… I'm so sorry that happened you," my home girl Juicie J comforted me at STK after I told her all about Eli attacking me. We had just finished eating lunch and had began to catch each other up on our lives. It had been three days since Eli raped me on my kitchen floor with my baby sitting right there. I was still pretty shook and I wanted him dead.

"So what's going on with your baby daddy?" She asked me, chanting the subject.

As soon as the words left her mouth, I saw his wife walk into the restaurant with my ex-boyfriend, Javi

"Oh my god!" I hissed as I peered around the column. I ducked low so that Javi wouldn't recognize me. Even though she didn't know who I was, he may have said something to me. I needed to remain incognito.

"What are you doing?" Juicie asked me.

"Shhhh and whisper. You see Javi over there?"

"Yea. Damn he look good!"

"Fuck that. You see the bitch he with?"

"The thick girl?"

"Yea. That's Braxton's wife."

"Oh really. Well, she sho' is friendly with Javi. That bitch got googly eyes while staring at him. I mean he is fine but what the hell is she doing with him?"

"I have no clue..." I replied before whipping out my phone. I needed to sneak and get a few shots of them together because this could be my ticket into the mayor's mansion. If he finds out that she is cheating he just might leave her for me.

"Do you want to leave?" J asked me while I kept my head low, peaking around dinner tables. They were sitting far enough to not see me. However, I could see them. Raising my phone I adjusted the zoom so that I could get a clear shot of them. It was very difficult because it was dark inside. And a flash would have brought attention to me.

"No. I need to see if they are going to kiss or something."

"Aight," Juicie replied before continuing to talk about something else. Instead of listening to her brainless rants about stripping at the Sweet Suite, I paid close attention to Javi and Braxton's wife.

What in the hell was he doing with her? He looked like he was into her. Actually, it looked like he was in love with her. I could see it in his eyes. Javi looked at her in a way I never saw him look at any woman, including me. I fucked with that nigga for six months. A wave of jealousy swept over me, making the muscles in my stomach tight. Two men that I have been with, loved her. What is it about her? She's pretty but the bitch is huge.

I watched as Javi bought her bottles of champagne and delicious food. Blood boiled in my veins because he never took me to a nice restaurant when we were together. It was the Waffle House after the club closed or a Chinese buffet. This nigga had steak and lobster with this woman.

I snapped photos of it all so that I could show Braxton. This bitch couldn't have both of my men!

"Mayeka, we been here for a minute. I'm ready to go. I gotta pick Man-Man from the daycare."

I heard her but for some reason, I couldn't tear my eyes away from the couple. They looked madly in love. Braxton doesn't take me out anywhere either. The more I thought about it, the more pissed I became.

And finally, Javi leaned and kissed the bitch. This picture would surely send Braxton over the edge. I snapped a picture of them kissing.

"Come on let's get out of here," I replied before easing away from the booth. While J and I walked out to the car, I texted Braxton the photos.

Me: Look at who I saw today.

* * *

"Where did you see them at?" Braxton interrogated me while we sat in the living room of my apartment. I held BJ closely in my arms while I watched him pace the floor. I had never seen him so angry in my life.

"At STK My girlfriend and I had lunch there. By the way it's a nice place. You should take me on a date there sometime," I interjected.

"Not now Mayeka! Shit. This is my wife!"

"And what am I?" I thrashed.

"Don't do this right now. You know how I feel about you. I love you with all of my heart. But you know this could hurt my damn campaign. Who else saw them?"

"Um the whole restaurant."

"You know what I mean. Did you show these pics to anyone else?"

"Nope. Just you," I replied while rolling my eyes.

"You need to delete them. No one else can see this."

"I thought you would be happy about this. This is clearly your way out of a marriage you don't want to be in…" MY voice trailed off as I readjusted my son in my arms.

"Why the hell would I be happy about this. You already know that I can't be with you right now. I need to win this damn election. My family bred me for this. And I need Cipriana by my side to get there. Fuck!" He interrupted his self.

"Just get out. I don't want you hear. Go home to your fat hoe of a wife. And by the way, the nigga that she is out in the open kissing in the mouth, he's a trap nigga. That's right, he sells drugs!"

"Mayeka, baby, I'm sorry. I really am. And you gotta know I appreciate you doing this for me. I will make this up to you. But right now I have to go handle some business."

"Whatever, Braxton," I said waiving him off while he approached the door.

"I'm going to make this up to you. And thank you so much. I have to fix this before it gets out," Braxton replied as he opened the door and walked out.

Angrily, I stood from my couch and placed BJ down in his crib. I had to do something. If those pictures weren't enough for him to leave the bitch, then there had to be something else I could do. Cipriana needed to go. I would stop at no costs to get my man and have him for myself. I needed to be protected and shielded from Eli and the only way to have that was to have him in the house full time.

I'm about to go to war with this bitch. I needed my man home with me.

Chapter 23

Aria

Hair slicked back in a bun, dress cradling my curves and face twisted in judgement, I rolled through the Sweet Suite for my husband's pool grand opening. Nokio and I decided that we had to act as natural and normal as possible until we exacted our plan to kill Czar.

"Wassup up Aria," Javi greeted me when I strolled past him.

I gave him a faint waive and kept it moving.

"You so damn boujee," he spat. Damn right I was. I had no desire to communicate with the people the worked for my husband.

"Aria what are you doing here?" Czar asked me when he saw my making my way through the room.

"I'm here to support my husband," I responded. I must admit he did look incredibly sexy today in his shorts and white linen button up. A pair of Gucci shades covered his eyes making it difficult to see the expression behind them.

"We haven't spoken in damn near weeks. Don't come in here starting any shit."

"We haven't spoken in weeks because you refuse to come home."

"And who's fault is that?" He sneered.

"Sorry to interrupt, Czar. Kareem told me that the cases of Ciroc were stashed in your office. I need to get those," some random bitch said. She completely ignored that I was even there.

"Ahem," I cleared my throat, making my presence known

"I'm sorry…"

"Cola this is my wife. Aria this is Cola Caine our new bartender." I sized the chocolate woman up and down. She was cute but not as fly as me of course. However, she looked very familiar. I couldn't put my finger on where I had seen her but I knew I had seen her somewhere.

"Nice to meet you."

"Yea, yea," I replied.

"Damn Aria why do you have to be so rude?!"

I sucked my teeth and rolled away to the bar where Kareem was serving drinks. I couldn't wait to get rid of Czar. He was becoming disrespectful anyway. He poured me several shots and I took them to head to help me let loose.

"You ok?" Nokio asked me from behind.

I wasn't but now that he was here, things were going to change.,

* * *

Apryl

I couldn't believe that rude ass woman was Czar's wife. Seeing how snooty she was explained why he hadn't forgiven her for aborting his child. Subconsciously he may have been looking for a way out considering how insufferable she was.

"You gotta excuse my wife, she doesn't have any manners," Czar spoke while I followed him from the outside to his office.

"It's all good. I get it. You're the king so the queen thinks she can talk down to your subjects," I joked.

"Don't say shit like that. You're not my subject. Shit, you've done more for my business in a month then she's done in a long time. I know I forgot to tell you this but you did a really good job on this party. Thank you." He winked at me before opening up his door.

"You're welcome," I replied.

"Have you started applying for schools?" He asked me while he unlocked the closet to his office.

"Not yet." God, I hated that I was lying to him especially since he genuinely cared. More importantly I felt all kinds of conflicted about what was going on in my life. From finding out my husband was cheating to finding out my brother in law ran him over; I was fucked up.

And then to top it all off, I had to do right by Nino or he could ruin my life. All of this shit muddles my feelings I have for Czar. They were intense. I cared about him and wanted him. Cheating on my husband had never been an option until I found out he was cheating go me.

"Here it is. I'll carry it outside for you," Czar stated when he discovered the heavy box of liquor bottles.

"Thank you."

"Cola, you have to apply for school and do it soon. Don't you want to enroll for the fall semester? It's already close to being summer," he said as he locked the door behind us.

"I know. I'm waiting on a few recommendation letters."

"True. Let me know if you have any issues with that."

It ate at me that he cared about me going to college. I wish I could tell him the truth. But if I didn't bust this case, I would never get promoted.

Once we arrived back out by the pool, Czar unloaded the boxes and I got back to work. His wife was talking to a group of people by the edge of the water with a drink clutched in her hand.

She spoke so loud, that I could hear her from across the way. What in the hell did Czar see in her? He must've been asking himself that question because as he stared at her he should his head in disappointment.

"Ay what's up with Aria?" Javi asked him when he walked up to him.

"I don't know. I think she is just showing out because I haven't been home in a minute."

"No. I don' think you understand what I'm asking you. Look at her. Does something seem strange?"

Following, Javi and Czar's gaze, I stared at Aria to see what Javi was referring to. And when I looked a little harder, I was able to see it. This lying bitch!

"Yo... her toes are moving," Javi concluded. "You see them shits wiggling in her toes. The bitch got so drunk that she can move her feet."

"What the fuck?!" Czar mouthed.

"When was the last doctor's appointment of hers that you've been too?" Javi asked. I tried to pretend as if I weren't eavesdropping by tending to the partygoers, but it was damn near impossible. It was as if I could feel the earth shaking, the sky shattering and a life ending storm brewing. Czar was probably about to kill this bitch in front of everyone.

"It's been almost a year. She would always schedule the appointment when I had to be out of town or something. Fuck! This bitch been faking it?" Czar said through gritted teeth.

"Don't do nothing crazy," Javi warned but by then it was too late...

Czar marched over to Aria's wheelchair as if he were about to choke the life out of her. The people who were standing around her scattered about like roaches when the lights are turned on.

"What are you doing?!" Aria asked when Czar viciously grabbed her wheel chair and pushed it towards the pool.

He ignored her. The entire party grew silent as they looked at them. She turned around and began hitting him to stop him from doing the unthinkable. But he kept on pushing her towards the deep end because he had a point to prove.

"NO!!!"

* * *

Aria

"I saw you move your feet!" Czar shouted out.

"Um no you didn't!"

Damn it, it looked like my secret was out.

Czar towered over me, gripping my wheel chair tightly and driving me towards the pool.

"What the hell are you doing?" I shouted.

"You haven't invited me to doctor's appointment in over a year. The shit is all becoming clear. You're a fraud ass bitch."

"What the hell are you talking about?"

"YOU GOT ME FUCKED UP!" He growled.

Inch by inch, he pushed me to the deep end of he pool. Finally he threw the entire wheelchair into the water, wheel chair and all. The water slapped against my face hurt as if someone had actually ran a wet palm across my cheek. My body hit the surface creating a splash before I sank to the bottom. There goes my suede Giusepes and not to mention my weave.

A part of me wanted to stay there and drown, rather than admit that for the past year I had been lying about not being able to walk.

Yep. I lied. At first it was to make Czar feel bad and guilt him into giving me the world; which he did. Then it transformed into me loving the attention. Everywhere I went, people catered to me like I was a needy child. The attention gave me a new lease on life.

As my body struggled in the water, bubbles seeped out of my nose. I could feel my head getting light, which meant I was going to pass out. The fact that no one had jumped into save me meant Czar was telling them not too.

Fuck it. I needed to get out the pool. I wasn't going to die like this.

A chorus of gasps spilled out of the crowd as I emerged out of the pool. They were all looking on at the spectacle.

"AHHH!" I gasped for air as I swam to the top. The only faces I could recognized through my chlorine blurred vision was Nokio, Javi and Czar who were all shaking their heads at me.

"It's a miracle! I swear it's a miracle!" I shouted, still grasping for straws, hoping that someone would believe me. The entire party stood around watching me as I struggled to swim to the ledge and pull myself out. Yep. I had been faking being handicapped this entire time. Shit would have worked I hadn't gotten so wasted.

Since I rarely walked, I had lost a lot of muscle tone therefore my legs were wobbly as I climbed up the pool's stairs.

"It's a miracle. I can walk!" I shouted hoping people would believe me but they all stood around shaking their heads.

Czar charged towards me as if he were about to throw my ass back into the pool but Javi caught him.

"Don't do this. Not right here," Javi said through gritted teeth.

"Baby I swear it's a miracle," I whined.

"Shut the fuck up. Yo Nokio take this bitch the warehouse and wait with her until I get there. Don't let her leave or do anything!" Czar instructed.

I bit my cheek to ensure that I didn't grin. If only he knew that having Nokio take me anywhere wasn't a threat to me it, it was a treat.

"I'm sorry," I lied as Nokio grabbed me by the wrists.

"Yea you're sorry piece shit. Get this hoe out of here," he instructed Nokio.

"Come on, Nokio whispered in my ear," as he carried me away.

Luckily we were close to killing Czar. I wasn't worried about a thing. I would have to apologize for lying to Nokio but he'd get over it eventually.

Chapter 24

Apryl

"This shit is over. Everybody get the fuck out," Czar announced before rushing out of the party. Everyone stood around looking confused for a moment.

"Yo he said get the fuck out!" Javi reiterated. The crowd shuffled about, collecting their things to head out. Women slid back into their jeans after drying off. Fellas paid their tabs before bouncing. Folks were in such a rush, that of course no one tipped the bartender.

Thirty minutes later the pool area cleared, leaving just Javi, myself and Kareem to clean up the mess the party made.

"That shit was wild," Kareem while packing bottles of liquor into crates so that we could move them back inside.

"Hell yea it was. I can't believe that bitch!" Javi commented while picking up garbage.

"She always been a spoiled brat, but to fake like her legs didn't work. That's taking it way too far. You don't think he's going to kill her do you!"

"Nigga!" Javi admonished Kareem for speaking about killings in front of me.

"I meant in a figurate way," Kareem tried to play it off.

"I would understand. I couldn't imagine what I would do if I were betrayed like that," I chimed in.

That was the truth. A part of me was so hurt and heartbroken by the Nichelle and the Andre ordeal that I wanted to go to the hospital and rip his breathing tube out. Of course I wouldn't do that, but I was angry. So I knew that Czar was feeling all types of anger for that bitch.

"Ay Cola, take this cash box to Czar's office," Javi asked me.

I grabbed the cash box and made my way into the club. As expected Czar's office door was closed. Nervously, I knocked on the door to gain access.

"Who the fuck is it?" He barked.

"It's Cola," I spoke just above a whisper.

"Come in," he responded.

"Here's the money the bar made from the pool party tonight," I said placing the box on his desk and walking away.

"Thanks. You don't have to rush out of here," he said, stopping me in my tracks.

"I do. I have to set up the bar for tonight. The club re-opens in a couple of hours."

"I know. I just wanted to apologize for you having to see that side of me out there. I loved her at one point. To know she was lying to me at something this huge, on top of the abortion, got me fucked up."

"Betrayal is a hard pill to swallow," I said, thinking about my husband's transgressions.

"I just hate liars. And I hate that I shared my bed, my home, my empire with a lying ass bitch like her."

Every time he said he hates liars, I just knew that my ass was lumped into to that.

"I know. You don't deserve that. But you have to wait until you calm down before you confront her again. You threw her in the pool in front of an audience. She could have died."

"Yea, that was stupid. I was just pissed the fuck off." He stood up from his desk and walked over to me.

"It's all good. Just be careful from here on out," I said as I attempted to walk away again even though I wanted to stay. I wanted to lay his head on my titties and tell him it was going to be ok. I wanted to tell him the truth about my husband so that he could tell me the same thing.

"Why you always running away from me? You scared of me?" he asked while licking his bottom lip.

"No," I whispered.

"What is it then?"

"Well you're my boss and you're married."

"Baby girl you saw what the fuck just happened…"

"I know but…"

"But what?" He cut me off, looking at me seductively. Why was I running from him? I had already dug myself into a hole so deep that I wasn't sure how I was going to get out of. And finding out that Kaz was cheating didn't make me feel any better.

Everything I did, I did for that man. It was time I did something for myself.

"But nothing," I replied before he leaned into kiss me. Before continuing, he broke away to make sure that his door was locked.

His presence made my heart beat out of chest and my pussy moisten on command. The ceiling fan above us whirled the scent of his cologne and my perfume through the room.

Finally after weeks of us, locking eyes and flirting, Czar pressed his lips to mine. Parting my lips with his tongue, he kissed me passionately before backing me into his desk. Unwilling to control my desire for him any longer I wrapped my arms around his neck and kissed him back.

Fuck Kazman. I know two wrongs don't make a right but this felt to good. Czar's hands crept up my dress and he pulled it off, tossing it to the side. Then he grabbed my ass, pressing his finger tips into my flesh as if he were gripping melons to test if they were ripe.

"You know how long I've wanted this?" I whispered in my ear.

"Tell me."

"Since the first day you pranced into the club," he replied before ripping my panties off of me.

"You know you're replacing those, right?" I giggled.

"You know I got you," he answered before sinking his teeth into my shoulder.

A moan dripped from my lips. This was really happening. It had been so long since I had been touched since Kaz had been in the hospital. And now that I know he was fucking Nichelle, I knew it would I never let him touch me again.

"Fuck me baby!" I groaned as he undid my bra before turning around. He violently swept everything off of his desk. Papers, files, pens and stapler all went plunging onto the floor.

Arching my spine, I tooted my ass to the air to give him greater access to my juice box. He pressed my body on to the desk, the smooth cool surface against my breasts, calmed the heat rising within me. I bit my bottom lip as my pussy quivered. I didn't need any four play. The passion had me juicy already.

"Damn you're so sexy," he complimented while taking his clothes off.

My hands reached behind me to feel him. First my fingers glided over his rock solid abs before finding his big dick. Gawdamn! This nigga was hung. How could his wife ever mistreat him? His dick alone would have been enough to make me act right. And to top it off he was giving her anything that she wanted.

"Tell me you want that dick!" he commanded as my fingers curled around his pulsating shaft.

"I want that dick right now!" I moaned.

Grabbing me by my waist he slid inside of me. "Ahhh!" I sung. It was pleasure and pain wrapped into one sexy package. My pussy could barely handle him, but I relaxed and let him fill my sugar walls.

"Shit. You are so fuckin' tight!" He moaned as he began to give me long deep strokes. I lay sprawled out on his desk as he swiveled in and out of of me. With each stroke he pressed against my g-spot making my pussy tremble.

"Yes!" I screamed as he began to plunge in and out of me with no mercy. He held tightly on my hips with one hand while slapping my ass with the other. The sting only intensified the feelings firing through my nerve endings.

Outside of his office I could hear that more people were coming into the club, dancers, patrons and other workers. If they knew what was going on behind closed these closed doors, it would look poorly on me. To them I would I just be some bartending thot getting fucked by the owner of the club.

"Keep going, harder," I cried while using my ninja grip around his dick. I squeezed the tip of his cock every time he entered me which magnified my orgasmic experience.

He ran his fingers through my wig and then pulled at my hair with authority. But, he gripped it so tightly that he tore the damn thing off my head.

"Shit!" I screamed as I grasped at his hand trying to put the wig back on.

"Fuck that shit. Stay still and focus on this dick not your hair!" he barked before throwing my wig to the side.

Choosing to stay in the moment, I did just that; focused on his dick. Before I knew it were both reaching our apex. His hands were entangled in my dreadlocks while my fingers were clawing at the smooth desk, trying to grip on something but it was no use.

"Come for me he demanded!"

"Yes daddy," I cried as I began to explode all over his dick.

"AHHH!" I screamed while my body convulsed against the table.

"Fuck!" He spat as he pulled his dick out of me and came on my ass.

"Damn girl, you got some bomb ass pussy," Czar complimented when he slid his dick off of me. Biting down on my bottom lip my body quivered against the cool surface of his desk. *What in the hell did I just do? Sure I was pissed at my husband but this wasn't right. As soon as we finished the guilt hit me like a ton of bricks.*

When he backed away from me so that he could get dressed, I lifted off of the desk and began to gather my clothes. Torn panties there, bra here, beads from my belly chain everywhere. What a guilty mess. If someone were to walk in here right now and see this, they would know exactly what happened. The messy clothes and the steam left on his desk painted a clear enough picture.

"Thanks," I breathlessly chuckled. "Please don't tell anyone about this," I continued while searching for my wig that he had snatched off in the throes of passion. In the next few moments I had to be back tending bar before I was missed.

"Are you looking for this?" Czar asked, holding up the auburn wig that usually hid my illustrious dread locks.

"Yeah," I replied, reaching my hand out.

Playfully he snatched it away. "I like your hair without it. I love dreads," he replied. Once more I reached for the wig dangling from his fingers. Instead of handing it over, he grabbed my arm and pulled me into his embrace.

"Come on and stop playing. There's a full house out there tonight. I don't want to get caught."

"Fine," he teased before kissing me on my cheek and then letting go.

"You look better with your dreads," he said as he gave me the wig.

"Thanks." I fixed it back on to my head. I walked away to continue to look for my clothes.

While I was busy looking for my strip-club bartender wear he had already pulled up his boxers and jeans. He swaggered around his office trying to locate his shirt. I couldn't help but watch his back muscles flex as he lifted up items to check for his shirt.

What the hell am I doing? I shook my head and tried to snap back to reality. This was the biggest mistake I had ever made. I had broken all of the rules. This shit could cost me everything, down to my life.

Here I am, a **married** undercover cop fucking the man I'm investigating. I'm having sex with the man I've been spying on and investigating. I knew he was trouble from the moment I laid eyes on him. If anyone found out about this, I could get fired. And if we arrest him, he will certainly tell my bosses we fucked. This could jeopardize the entire case. Why did in the hell did I do this?

"You ok?" he asked. The concern in my eyes must have been like graffiti sprayed on my face.

"Yes, just please don't tell anyone. I'd hate for your wife to find out," I tried to guilt him.

"Listen, I understand why you don't want me to say anything. I own this club and it would make shit difficult for you if they knew we were fucking. It'll be our little secret." Czar walked towards me and pulled me in, planting a kiss on my forehead.

"This is the first and only time this is happening." I snatched my body away. My words came from my mind but my body knew that I was lying. How in the hell could I stay away from a man like this. I was ashamed to admit that making love to him was better than with my husband

"Don't do me like that," he grinned. Damn he was fine. But there is no way I could ever let this happen again. If my husband finds out he will divorce me.

And what kind of wife am I? My husband was laying up in a coma for the last few months and here I was fucking in the back of strip club. It was bad enough I took this assignment without telling him and now this? I could lose him. I could lose my job and go to jail.

"I'm serious. I'm only here to bartend and make money. I aint here to be fucking you. Those other strippers will make life hell for me if they knew. You know they all want you."

"Well, you're the only one that I want."

"Uh huh. I told you this was a one time thing. Besides you are married!" I spat while putting the finishing touches on my look.

His jaw flexed and he shook his head. "Fuck my wife," he replied. Just as he did someone knocked on the door.

"Shit!" murmured.

Who in the fuck was it? This was just thing I didn't need. I surely didn't need a witness to my transgressions.

They knocked once more. This time Czar went to answer it. I looked around for a place to hide but it was too late.

"Ay." To my relief, it was Javi standing on the other side of the door. He shook his head at the realization that Czar and I just fucked. The evidence was all over the floor.

"Wassup."

"There's someone out there here to see Cola. They said its very important."

My face scrunched in disbelief. Who could be here wanting to speak with me? Trying to pull myself together, I walked outside to find that it was Andre waiting for me. My stomach dropped to soles of my feet. What in the hell could he possibly want from me? He knew it was against protocol to show up here like this.

"Hey Jessica," Andre greeted me by my undercover name.

"What's going on?" I asked looking straight at Andre.

"Kaz died.," Andre answered.

My jaw hit the ground. I was in shock and didn't know how to respond.

Chapter 25

Cipriana

The children were fast asleep in their room and I was preparing to do the same. Of course, it was another night and Braxton wasn't home. After making love to Javi on his pool table, I came to the realization that I didn't need Braxton. I just want to be done with him and get out of this marriage. With the money I'd get by selling my rights to SanRo, I could definitely take care of myself. I can always write a new book and invest some of the money into marketing that. The more I thought about it, the more I realized I didn't need that nigga at all.

I laid down and scrolled through my phone to see that I received a text message from Javi.

Javi: My pool table still smells like you.

Me: Boy stop…

Javi: It does. When you comin' back over?

Me: You know I got this situation. I don't want to make it messier. I need to leave Braxton. I don't want to continue with you while still being here.

Javi: True. Well I gotta get some work done. Hit me in the morning.

I slid my phone onto my nightstand and closed my eyes to get some rest. While I wasn't sure where this was going with Javi, I knew I could't stay with Braxton. He was far too disrespectful. I don't want to rush into anything with Javi but I need to rush out of this marriage. With thoughts of my divorce on my mind, I began to drift off to sleep.

* * *

CRASH!

"What the hell!?" I called out when I heard a loud sound, jolting me out of my sleep. After the crash I began to smell smoke. Once my senses adjusted I was able to hear my smoke detectors going off.

"FIRE!" I could hear Robyn shout to loudly.

"Mommy help us!" The girls screamed outside of my door. I raced out of bed so that I could see what was happening. But when I approached my door, I couldn't get it open. It was locked.

"I'm coming baby, go back to your room! Get your sisters and stay away from the smoke," I called out to them.

"It's everywhere!" Robyn shouted back at me.

"PLEASE HELP!" They screamed.

I tried my damnedest to get the door open but it wouldn't budge. Panic ensued. My throat tightened and my entire body began to sweat. I had to save my daughters.

"God! Please help us!" I cried out trying to open the door.

I searched the room and could find nothing. The kids cried in the hallway and before I knew it, smoke was seeping underneath my door into my room. I grabbed a t-shirt to over my mouth and nose and began to rush the door

I slammed my body into the door several times, hoping that I could get to them. God don't let this fire take my babies from me!

* * *

Ready for Episode 2?

Sign up here to be notified! This will be released in June!

Like us on FB for updates + giveaways!

Join our FB group!

Free Book Excerpt #1

Ratchet Wives Club: Orignal

If someone had told me I would be on my knees ready to suck dick for crack, I wouldn't have believed them. If they would've said "Michaela, you will be kneeling at the dick of one of your husband's rivals at your best friend's divorce party, begging to suck his dick for an 8 ball," there is no way I would believe them. Fuck no. Not me, the Howard Law graduate who is a partner in her firm at only 29 years old. Oh hell no, not me, the sexy bitch with the amazing husband and the most adorable five year old daughter.

No way in hell, I thought I would ever find myself in this crazy ass predicament. It's funny the places life can take you. Life will chew you up and vomit you out, with absolutely no mercy. It will have you ready to give head, just for a high. A high that has become my greatest escape from the deep secrets I've been holding from husband and the rest of my family. And now, I'm down here in my satin black BCBG dress, fiendin' for crack.

"Bitch, hurry up! I don't have time to wait on yo' ass," Bobby snapped, while looking down at me. The raspiness in his voice caused my arms to dot with goose bumps. I was nauseous from the intense withdrawal I as going through. And the floral scent of the air freshener didn't help.

I was hesitating to put my mouth of that nigga's dick. Shit, my husband was on the other side of that door out in the party waiting for me. But I swear to god if I didn't get high, I would die.

"Yea, I got you," I hissed, tugging at his waistband trying to find his dick. This can't be life. I need help because this shit has gotten way out of hand. After this next high, I'm done. I'm getting help because if my husband finds out about this, that nigga will kill me.

My knees ached against the marble floor as I unzipped his jeans and took out his flaccid dick. This shit ain't even hard yet. Ew! Whipping out his dick, I stuck the small and soft as a noodle thingy, in my trembling mouth. If I can just get through this, I can get a hit and be out of here.

Finally, he started to get hard, while I bobbed my head and forth. My heart was beating so quickly I felt it would jump out of my chest and onto that ground. Peeping up at him, I could see that his eyes were closed and he was in ecstasy. I wasn't even putting my all into it, not like I did with my husband, Cameron.

When I'm with Cameron, I give him that bomb head. My mouth gets soaking wet, while I deep throat him and look into his eyes. I swallow his nut like it's a milkshake on a blazin' summer day, because I love him.

But with Bobby, I half-assed it. Mouth dry as ash and I didn't use my tongue nor perform none of the theatrics I usually do. He didn't seem to mine because with in a matter of moments, he busted his nut.

He tilted my head back and he squirted all over my perfectly beat face. Disgusting. That warm and sticky shit ran down my face and dripped onto the ground while he stood there laughing at me. I shuttered as tears trickled down my cheeks, swirling in his mess.

"Here ya go. Clean ya self up before that nigga sees you," he chuckled, tossing the crack on the ground. Unlocking the door, he scurried out of there, while I rushed to the baggy on the floor.

I clutched it to my chest and rocked it like it was a newborn baby. Tears poured from my exhausted eyes because finally I could get

high. This was not my life, just a month ago. What started as a recreational coke snorting habit, turned my sadiddy ass into a crack-head.

Read the rest for **FREE!**

Free Book Excerpt #2

Ashes to Ashes Dust to Side Chicks

Chapter 1

Nova

"You just need to leave him," I flatly said to Misa, while swirling pasta around my fork before stuffing it in my mouth.

"I can't! You know I can't." She sniffled, barely touching her lunch.

There we sat outside at Luciano's, an Italian eatery in downtown D.C., eating lunch and talking about her philandering husband.

Misa was a beautiful woman, but since getting married and spitting out a few babies, she had let herself go. I remembered telling her, she had to keep it tight, if she didn't want that fine ass husband of hers to look outside of home for some pussy.

But she didn't listen. She swore up and down he loved her for who she was no matter what.

My response was, "What does love have to do with his dick?"

Men can love you and still want to fuck other bitches. Your job is to keep him so satisfied so that he is too caught up in you to sleep around.

But Misa didn't keep up with her looks to keep him interested. And what the hell was her excuse? It wasn't like she had to work. My ass worked, sometimes 60 hour work weeks. And I still managed to keep my body looking good, hair done, food on the table, and pussy or mouth on his dick. Granted, I had no kids yet, but work took up just as much time.

"I just can't believe he would do this to me! I supported him through law school! If it weren't for me, he wouldn't even be an assistant district attorney. And he does this to me!" Her tears had dried, but the anger still lingered.

I paused from scarfing down the fettuccine alfredo that lay on my plate to look her in her sad eyes.

She had a cute round face, the color of burnt sienna. Her skin was so smooth and unblemished; it looked as if she were wearing foundation. But that was the only thing she had going for her.

The three babies she popped out for her asshole husband had left her skinny-fat. She never had much boobs or butt, but the babies made everything sag. Her naturally long hair was never done. She kept it swooped in a ponytail. And she stayed in baggy t-shirts and unflattering yoga pants.

I had tried to tell her before, but it never worked. And now wasn't the time. What she needed now was encouragement.

"Just leave him, Misa. You are beautiful, talented, and intelligent. You don't need him."

"I can't leave him. The kids are in really good daycares and I can't afford it without him. Where will I live? What will I drive? You know I signed a pre-nup."

Shaking my head, I took a sip of the ice water in my glass. Women were so dumb. This was why I could never be fully dependent on a man.

Sure, my husband and I were a power couple. But if he left, I would be okay. You had to have a career and never ever sign a pre-nup! If he cheated, you needed to be taking his ass to the cleaners.

"Is he only cheating with one girl? And do you know who it is?" I prodded.

"Yeah, that I know of. She's the only one who's been texting him and calling him. I finally followed him one day, and he went to a hotel to see her."

"You have to get rid of her. Just kill her ass," I joked while laughing. It lightened the mood, forcing Misa into giggling.

"I wish. That little bitch knows he's married yet she still runs around with him."

"I hate those kind of women! Side chicks and mistresses. Get your own man, you pathetic broads!" I fussed.

I really did hate those bitches. They break up homes every day. I know it's really the man's fault, but if there weren't so many of those hoes who willingly slept with married men, there wouldn't be nearly as big of a problem.

Sometimes, I wished all of those bitches would just die. I know that's terrible. I need help, pray for me. I laughed to myself.

"Well girl, I know you have to get back to work. I don't want to hold you up."

"Yeah, let me head back to the office so I can wrap up this press release. Maybe we can catch up this weekend for a spa day?" I suggested. With all the stress she was dealing with, she needed it.

"I'll see if I can get someone to watch the kids."

"Let me know," I replied, while we waited for the check to come.

* * *

After lunch, I sashayed down the crowded sidewalk to get back to my building. My leopard Loubous clicked along the cement, while I switched my curvy ass. Niggas broke their necks to catch a glimpse of the fat ass walking before them.

I was a naturally thick girl. In spite of some of the cosmetic surgery I had I was definitely still considered a BBW. Right after college, I went and got liposuction around my midsection and had the fat transferred to my tits and my ass, giving me a bodacious hour-glass figure. I was thick in all the right places.

My butter pecan skin was flawless and glinted underneath the sun as I trekked back to my office. The black pencil skirt I wore hugged my hips, but the tan blouse I wore was much more modest.

I couldn't be in my office with my cleavage showing. My goal was to eventually become one of the vice presidents at the public relations firm. And I wasn't going to get there dressing like one of these thots.

"Welcome back Ms. Shelton," Ron, the security guard greeted me as I walked through the halls. He was always nice to me, trying to flirt.

"Hey Ron. And you know its Mrs., right?" I corrected him. I don't play that shit. I'm a married woman who is deeply in love with my man. I rock this diamond on my fourth finger with pride.

"Excuse me! I was just wishful thinking," he joked. Without verbally responding, I smirked and stepped on the elevator to the 12th floor, where I had my own office with a beautiful view of the city.

At only twenty-eight years old, I had made senior account executive at the firm, Ashworth Marketing. Which allowed me to lead some PR and marketing campaigns for a lot of heavy hitters that included beverage brands, apparel companies, and real estate.

Before going back into my lovely office, I stopped in the restroom to reapply my cherry colored lipstick. While in the bathroom, I primped my hair, which was cut in the mushroom bob style, similar to Rihanna's.

I went to my hairdresser weekly to keep the hairstyle looking perfect. I don't know who made up the lie that short hair was less maintenance. When you have a style like this, you have to keep your kitchen looking good.

After assuring my hair was perfect and my lips were on fleek, I settled back at my desk to complete the day.

"Hey Nova," Andrea, my manager, a vice president, said when she walked into my office.

"Hi Andrea, what's going on?"

"I just wanted to give you a kudos for the lovely job you did on the American leg of the Satori campaign. The stuff is flying off the shelves all over the country." Andrea referred to Satori wine, a Japanese wine company that hired Ashworth to do its marketing.

It was my first assignment as an account executive, and I had done a really good job.

"Thank you! I read the reports this morning. The sales are doing well."

"It's all because of you. Keep up the good work, lady. One day soon you'll be up there with me and the other big dogs," she chuckled.

"You know that's always been the goal." I smiled.

"I know and you're well on your way. I'm rooting for you," she replied before turning away.

"Oh and before I forget. Your bonus will be in this next paycheck and I'm sure you will be pleasantly surprised." She winked before exiting.

There was nothing like doing an amazing job and getting paid for it. As I read over the press release that I wrote for another client, my cell phone rang. It was my mother, Antoinette, also known as Toni.

"Sup ma," I answered with the phone pressed between my ear and my shoulder.

"Nova, I need you to come over tonight. I have a surprise I want to tell the family. Bring your husband," she gleefully said.

"It's a little short notice, don't you think?"

"Just come. It's very important. You know, Nova, you only have one mother. You need to treat me right…" She went on her extended rant about how I should treat her well since she was older and could die tomorrow. Rolling my eyes, I blocked her out. I hated when she did that shit.

"Fine, I'll be there. I'll talk to you later," I replied. As soon as I hung up, I phoned my husband. I hated interrupting him at work. He didn't need any distractions. Just like me, he was also one of the youngest people at his job in an upper management position.

My baby worked for one of the top real estate development firms in the area, Durden Development. Like I said, we were a power couple, striving to be the best in our careers and lead elite lives.

"Hey sweetie," he answered the call.

"Good afternoon, love. I won't hold you. Please meet me at my mother's house tonight. She said she had an important announcement and wants you there along with me."

"What? Is she pregnant?" He laughed at his own joke.

"Boy please. She better not be. As old as she is." I laughed back.

"You said it, not me." He continued to chuckle.

"You implied it. But can I count on you to be there?"

"Of course. I love you. I gotta run."

"Love you too, baby." I hung up and returned to work.

I loved how my husband made an effort to be there for me.

* * *

Chapter 2 - Tyriq

"Of course. I love you. I gotta run," I replied before hanging the phone up on my gorgeous wife.

But when I looked up from my cell phone, I was met with an evil eye and severe sucking of teeth.

"Don't be like that," I said to Kinasha, my assistant and secret jump off.

"I just hate how you do that shit in front of me. You see me sitting right here, yet you still answer your phone when she calls. It's disrespectful," she hissed while poking her bottom lip out.

These thots never knew how to stay in their place. I cleared my throat and shrugged it off, while returning back to our conversation.

"What was I saying again? Oh yeah, I need you to come with me to the meeting tomorrow at the Gardens. I need you to be my eyes and ears. You take really good notes, okay?"

"Uh huh, I'll be there. But seriously, Tyriq, why are you even still with her? I thought we had something special," she whined while biting down on her bottom lip.

Every time she did that shit, my dick jumped. If we didn't have so much work to do, I would lock my office door and bend that ass over my desk, like I'd done hundreds of times.

"Because she's my wife," I flatly stated.

I know it sounds fucked up, but I do love my wife. But we got married too young and I'm not ready to stop getting pussy. I loved a variety of women. My wife was thick and had sexy short hair.

But Kinasha was petite with long hair. I loved tossing her little ass around and watching her tiny pussy swallow all ten inches of my dick. Her honey colored skin looked good against my deep chocolate flesh. Whenever I hit it from behind, I got to tangle my fingers in her hair while pounding her little pussy.

If she could shut up about my wife, we would be fine.

"I want to see you more, though. You get so busy..." she began to ramble.

"Fine, I'll make more time for you. You know you the best, baby. I care for you and love that pussy." I was careful to never say that I loved her, because I didn't. I was also careful to never give her money. What I made went back to my household with my wife.

"Oh, I know you do," she whispered, while spreading her legs so that I could catch a glimpse of her pink center.

"Damn, you better put that away. My door ain't locked."

"I don't give a fuck, let them watch." She sat across from my desk, rubbing her clit with one hand while sucking on her other finger. She simulated a blow job on her fingers, causing me to get rock hard.

"Seriously, Kinasha, go back to work. I'll break you off later."

"Fine, boss. I'll go back to work. But are you coming through tonight?"

"Nah, I have to go to a family thing."

There she went with that sucking her teeth shit. "You missed my birthday yesterday. And now you're telling me I can't see you tonight either?"

"We'll fuck again soon. And trust me, it will be worth the wait."

"Okay, baby," she said as she walked away.

Taking a few deep breaths, I waited for my dick to go soft so that I could get back to work. Durden Development was going through a lot of changes and if I wanted to continue to move up in the company I had to be able to rock with those changes.

I was on a mission to become partner in this company or open my own development firm. With my wife inspiring me, I made it through college and grad school at the top of my classes. And now I was making well over 100k.

It was as if we had it all: a mini mansion in Bowie, Maryland, three luxury cars between the two of us, a pair of Shih Tzus, and a timeshare in Jamaica. The only thing that was missing was children. Which didn't bother me much because I didn't think we had time for them yet.

Eventually, I want kids after I get this shit out my system. I can't stop fucking around and having kids would get in the way of that.

While I scanned the finance report on my computer screen, my office phone beeped. Looking at the caller ID, I could see that it was Kinasha.

"What's up," I greeted after pressing speakerphone.

"Cole Barnes is here to see you. I know he doesn't have an appointment, but he said it's urgent."

My temples throbbed at hearing his name.

"Send him back," I sighed. I did not feel like dealing with this nigga Cole, who I knew from the hood as Chop.

In a matter of moments the doorknob to my office turned and in walked the nigga from my sordid past.

"Wsup Chop." I stood and extended my hand to him.

He shook it before sitting down in the chair that Kinasha's sexy ass once sat in.

"Mr. Shelton! This is a nice set up you have going on here."

"Cut to it, why are you here?" I asked. I used to work the corners back in the day with Chop. We were both on the come up but now he was the kingpin. That could've been my life but I preferred to go straight. I'm too fucking pretty to be in prison. I used that drug money to pay for tuition and the rest is history.

"Damn nigga. I ain't seen you in a few years. Not since you got this cushy corporate job and that thick ass wife."

"Keep my wife out your fuckin' mouth," I barked.

"Whateva, nigga. I ain't come here for all of that. I came here because I need a favor."

"What kind of favor? I don't owe you shit."

"The hell you don't. It was my connect that helped you pay for grad school. If you didn't know me you woulda been broke and not able to even afford your degrees

that got you here."

He was right. He used to cop from one particular connect that used to keep us laced. I never got the opportunity to meet the connect but Chop was still doing business with him.

"Just get to it. What the hell do you want?"

"You know The Gardens over on the south side?" he asked, referring to some historic projects in the city.

"Yeah, my company working on putting a bid on that," I replied.

"I know, that's why I'm here. I need y'all to drop that shit."

"Nigga, have you lost your mind? You want us to drop our bid on that prime real estate?" I looked at him with confusion. The favor that he wanted me to perform was absurd.

"Yes, drop the bid. This gentrification shit is sucking the soul out of our city." He leaned into the chair, eyeing me like a hawk.

"Since when do you care about social issues? I thought all you were about is your dollas."

"That is all I'm about. I get a lot of my dollars from The Gardens. In fact, one of our traps is there. Which is why I need for no one to buy that property and build new fancy condos in its place."

Yep, this nigga had lost his mind.

"Chop, I can't help you. There's nothing I can do about The Gardens being sold." I shook my head as I eyed him.

He had an unnerving scar that ran down his cheek. To my knowledge, no one knew how he got the scar. But we all knew how he got the nickname.

When he was about 11, he caught his stepfather molesting his little sister. Later that night while the man was sleeping, Chop snuck into his room with a machete and severed his head.

He spent the next few years in juvi until he was 18. When he got out we started slinging together. But I went to college and later to grad school. Ain't no retirement plans for drug dealers. And I'm trying to live my life to its fullest.

"You can convince your company to drop the bid. So do it. I don't need any more explanations. I came in here and asked nicely. Don't let me get ugly," he barked.

"Quiet your damn voice. This is a place of business. All that shit might work in the trap but this is a company," I chastised him. I could see the fury brewing within him.

"Is no your final answer?" he questioned me as if I were going to change my mind.

"No is my final answer. That's not how shit works around here. Besides, I don't have the power to tell them to drop a bid that will bring the company tens of millions of dollars."

He tilted his head back and released an evil chuckle that eventually progressed to him clapping.

"Did I say something funny?" I thrashed. My patience had run thin and I wanted him out of my fuckin' office.

"Yeah, you funny. You one funny nigga," he said in between laughing.

"How is that?"

"You don't have no power. You moved all that weight back in the day just to become a monkey in a suit."

My abs tightened while my palms began to sweat. If I were light enough you would have been able to see my skin burn red. This nigga had the audacity to insult me, while I was out here trying to live a decent life.

"Well, what does it say about you that you have to come and ask a monkey in a suit for help," I slickly replied.

His face went stone cold.

"I would tread lightly if I were you."

"How about you tread your ass up out my office. This monkey in a suit has real work to do. Go back to the trap where your ass belongs."

Standing, he brushed his True Religion jeans to release any wrinkling. He let out a snicker that grated my nerves before replying.

"This won't be the last time you see me," he spoke before turning towards the door and heading out of my office.

Once he left, I let out a sigh of release. I knew not to ignore Chop's threats, but what could he really do to me? I knew too many of his secrets for him to try me. And I doubt if he would kill me because my brothers would react and blood would spill in these streets.

That nigga knows that. And he doesn't want a war.

I leaned back into my cushiony leather office chair and caught a glimpse of the photo that sat on my desk. It was a picture of Nova and me on our wedding day. She looked so beautiful that day and I vowed to give her whatever she wanted. Which reminded me, I had to get some more work done so I could go to her mother's house this evening.

Read the rest on Amazon. Ashes to Ashes Dust to Side Chicks

Free Book Excerpt #3

Killuminati

"That was him?" Brody asked when he stepped out of the shower.

"Yea. How is he just getting home? I thought you said you sent him to the Upper West Side. He should have been in the house." I replied before taking a sip of water. Brody slid his freshly clean body next to me before pulling me in.

"Maybe he's out doing what your ass is. Cheatin'," Brody chuckled. I sucked my teeth in response. I would break his neck if he cheated on me.

Yeah, I'm a hypocrite. I knew it was messed up to be sleeping with Dab's best friend and producer but lately all he does is work. If he's not in the street making money, he's in the studio with Gainz making music.

Ever since I gave birth to Keami, he's spent less and less time with me. When Brody started paying me attention I couldn't help but fall for it. Brody and I both knew that we were dead ass wrong and we were going to stop fucking with each other soon. We have too. I really do love Dab and I know that Brody has love for him as if he were his brother.

It's just that me and Brody had an intense connection and the sex was toe-curling, heart-palpitating good. Of course Dab hit it just right but Brody made me feel like he cared.

"We gotta stop this shit, ma'," Brody said out loud expressing my inner thoughts.

"I know."

"That's my brother. He really loves you and KeKe."

"I know. I swear this is the last time," I said, knowing that I was lying. Every time we get together we say that it's the last time and it never is. If Dab would stay at home sometime, he could be getting my pussy instead of Brody. If he would just love me right, I wouldn't be out here in bed with Brody. Shit, he didn't call me or notice I was missing until 3:00am.

I sucked my teeth as I thought about how he didn't get back in the house until this late. Brody wiggled from my clutch and began to roll up another blunt. Brody was fine. His mother was Puerto Rican and his father was from Trinidad. He had a beautiful copper complexion with a pair of green eyes. He stood at 6'1, just a couple of inches shorter than Dab. Brody's muscular medium build was decked out with various tattoos, including a tat of his son's name on his neck.

Brody and his baby mother been broke up because he cheated on her last year. Ever since then, the both of them had been in a custody battle for his seven-year-old son, Symir. She wanted child support but Brody worked under the table. I try to stay out of their business but Brody told me everything that he didn't feel like he can discuss with Dab. Even though they were close, those two men tried not to talk about their relationship drama.

"You not tired? You know you gotta go pick your baby and take her home in the morning," Brody spoke as he puffed on the blunt. He was right. I had to be up in about three hours to go get KeKe from my mother's house. She didn't know about Brody but she hates Dab.

"Yea I'm tired, but I want to get it one more time before I have to leave," I said sensually.

"Oh you want some more of this dick, huh?" He asked as he ashed the blunt.

I climbed on top of Brody's chiseled frame, letting him know I was serious. I was still naked from our previous tryst between the sheets. My body was one of the baddest in Uptown and it was natural too. My skin was butter pecan and I had big doe eyes with long lashes to match. I wore a bright red weave that cascaded down my back. I had a tribal tattoo on lower back, an arm sleeve tattoo of various things; including my grandmother's portrait, my daughter, butterflies and a sunset.

"Damn baby. Imma miss this when we're done," Brody whispered as his hands cupped my double d tits. Once he massaged my breasts he trailed his fingers down to my navel where he played with my belly button ring. My body was adorned with little surprises everywhere, from my hip and ass tattoo, to the piercing on my clit.

"I know," I murmured in his ear before I began to suck on his neck. The room was warm because the space heater was on 10 but we also had the ceiling fan spinning, circulating our sweet scents and the weed in the air.

Like most men, Brody had no sense of style when it came to interior decorating. We were lying on old gray sheets that had been washed so many times they were covered in lint balls.

Brody's fingers eased into my wet pussy before he reached for the condom. We always made sure to use protection. Neither one of us wanted anymore children nor did we want to complicate our arrangement any further.

He slid the condom over his dick, which was a nice size but not as big as Dab's. Once the rubber was secure I lowered my pussy onto him, his dick stretching me out. My walls gripped his girth as I began to ride him with no mercy.

"That's right. Give me that pussy baby," he demanded as I bounced my fat ass up and down on him. I arched my back and leaned forward and began working him like I was trying to make some money.

His hands pressed into my flesh as he dug deep in my pussy, surpassing my g-spot and forcing me to holler.

"AHHH!" I screamed when I felt him in my bellybutton.

"Yea, you wanted that. That nigga ain't doing you like this!" He spat before getting up and tossing me on my knees. He began to ram his dick in and out of me while slapping my ass. He reached to my weave to pull on it but I slapped his hand away. I spent too much time doing my hair for him to mess it up.

Instead of grabbing my weave, he gripped my hips with my both hands and began to smash into me. It hurt so good that I collapsed on to the old beady sheets and bit down on them. I knew that after we were done I would regret putting my mouth on those covers, Lord knows who else had been in his bed since Brody was a big hoe.

Before I knew it I began to cum all over his dick.

"That's right! Cum for daddy," he moaned as he stroked me long and hard. I could feel his dick pulse inside of me as he came. Breathing heavily, he pulled out of me with the condom still intact before he ran to the bathroom and flushed it before laying back down with me.

"I'm going to take a nap until 6:00am, then I have to get up," I replied while closing my eyes.

My pussy felt great and I was exhausted. I should've just taken my ass home tonight but I couldn't help myself.

* * *

"Yo! Wake up!" Brody said, shoving me violently. When I blinked my eyes open I could see that the sun was shining brightly which let me know that I had overslept. Brody had a look of panic written across his face as he started throwing clothes on quickly.

"What time is it?" I asked.

"It's 9:00am. My baby mother is about to drop of Symir and you're late pickin' up KeKe. You have to get out of here!" He barked, throwing my clothes at me. I jumped out of bed and put on my clothes and rushed out without peeing, brushing my teeth or washing my face. I felt disgusting but that was nothing compared to how I felt when I checked my text messages.

"WHERE THE FUCK ARE YOU?!" That was the only message I had from Dab. Immediately my heart raced while tears trekked down my face. This ain't good. As I walked down the street to my mom's house I noticed Brody's baby mother, Ayanna, walking up the street with Symir.

"Damn girl you look rough," she laughed.

"Crayz night." I replied.

"Well, take care of yourself. I have to go drop this little boy off," she said as she kept it moving. She didn't ask any questions and since I was a block away from Brody's apartment she didn't suspect anything. Luckily my mother lived a few blocks away. I would just pick up KeKe and tell Dab that I had overslept.

However, as I went through my phone I realized I had several calls from my mother. Shit!

Also By 5StarLit

Ran Off On The Plug Twice

Ratchet Wives Club: Original

Ashes to Ashes Dust to Side Chicks

Killuminati

Made in the USA
Middletown, DE
19 September 2018